Charlene & Zion
and Family

Red Sea

Pauline O'Reggio
Oct 2017

Red Sea

Leaving an Abusive Home

Comgin Rosemary

Library of Congress Control Number:		2016909113
ISBN:	Hardcover	978-1-5245-0775-6
	Softcover	978-1-5245-0774-9
	eBook	978-1-5245-0773-2

Print information available on the last page.

Rev. date: 07/28/2016

To order additional copies of this book, contact:
Xlibris
1-888-795-4274
www.Xlibris.com
Orders@Xlibris.com
733387

Contents

Dedication

To our Heavenly Father and Creator of all the Universes—thank you for delivering us from our Egypt and bringing us to a place to learn of you.

To my late grandparents—whose love and discipline gave me knowledge, understanding, and wisdom to survive and trust our Heavenly Father.

To my son:

Thank you for your kindness, forgiveness, love, and patience. I hope you never lose your sense of wonder. Promise me you will give life a fighting chance. I hope you will dance for joy each day as your relationship with the Lord grows.

To the shelters for men and women:

Thank you for your great work in helping families in directing them on the right path for healing. Thank you for helping save our lives.

To the men and women who are enduring this pain, the pain is real. We often believe we are alone and that no one cares and understand, but there are people who do. Do not be discouraged you will heal.

Note

After leaving the abusive home, I was extremely angry, quiet, and could not speak. While attending group meetings with other abused women, I listened to their stories, and felt their pain. Many cried with them, I could not, but deep inside I was very angry for all the hurt they endured and felt proud of their courage for leaving.

Some left their spouses because of misunderstandings, and others felt their lives were in grave danger. Unfortunately, due to my intense anger at the time, to this day, I cannot remember any details of their real stories. A friend once entreated me to write and express the real pain of abuse people are enduring and teach them how to leave and heal. After the first few years of healing I was convinced she was correct.

My message is a one-to-one, heart-to-heart communication with the reader, to help everyone who knows a victim of abuse, is experiencing abuse, or had experienced abuse continue to heal and help others to heal. It is a painful road to take that is less traveled but worth taking to reach your goal—true healing and growth, and a deep connection with our Father in Heaven.

Statistics regarding domestic violence worldwide corroborate the facts that no class, race, or color of people in society is exempt from this evil. From the richest to the poorest, from the least to the most educated experience this pain.

If you are been abused or know anyone been abused, contact your local authorities, shelters, counselors, medical professionals, police, or a lawyer in your local area for help and advice.

Introduction

The experience of the multitude of slaves' estrangement from their own land into Egypt, and their enslavement and escape (**Genesis 37–Exodus 40**) was chosen to help parallel some experiences of abused individuals while living in and escaping abusive environments.

Their experience of estrangement into exile from their own country, and some of their experiences returning to their homeland; the fears, doubts, anxieties they experienced are the same experiences of abused individuals exiting their abusive homes to a new beginning. Although the experiences of the multitude of slaves are different for some nations who had over the centuries experienced this pain in various degrees, it is abuse all the same.

Writing this book is an attempt to show all individuals experiencing abuse, while not unique to any nation, is extremely dark and sorrowful.

Thesaurus English (United States) defines abuse:

Definition of abuse*: mistreatment; misuse; insults; treat badly; insult; exploit; neglect.*

Abuse is a kind/type of behavior that person(s) engages in to unjustly control another person.

Abuse in its true context is often misunderstood and undermined by many people on all levels of society. Many people continue to grossly misrepresent right character, and in turn abuse others; thereby giving license to the abusers and re-victimizes the victims.

The Heavenly Father, our Creator, sees it differently, and is greatly appalled by it and will not stand by and watch you defenselessly struggle through life. As you will see He not only fiercely defends a great multitude of slaves against abuse, but also individuals against other abusers.

There are overwhelming examples in the Bible where He will fiercely defend the defenseless. He does, against popular beliefs, defend the fatherless and the widows: **Deuteronomy 10:18**—execute judgments of the fatherless; **Zechariah 7:10**—not to oppress the widow or the fatherless; **James 1:27**—pure faith . . . to visit the fatherless and widows. In **Psalm 68:5** He is the father of the fatherless, and a judge of the widows. There are many more examples of His protective care. Many people are cruel in nature and behavior and are openly speaking against children with no fathers. Yet He says—*I am the Father of the fatherless.*

Many individuals have great difficulties understanding abuse. Many never experienced it nor care to empathize with anyone who had experienced it. They try to theorize it out to nothing, while it is all up in their head—nothing but a guess game. Most do not know the true meaning of the word divorce in its true context and will try to cause you to feel at odds or guilty for escaping the abuser.

An abusive environment is not limited to home, groups, color of people, nationality, custom, economic status, nor education. It is worldwide. It exists in every kind of relationships, every country, city, town, street, and even in the workplace and religious communities.

This book is an attempt to help you identify the many kinds of abuse and its many traumatic affects and help you get the message that you were created to love and be loved. Families need to bond close to help create safer communities for all. You will see that you do have the authority and power to stand up against this falsehood call—abuse.

No one should isolate themselves when faced with this situation, whether they are the warning signs or the actual full-blown situations. Neither should the victims or witnesses allow themselves to relinquish and transfer their rightful authority and power to the abuser. You as the victim have more power and authority over this situation than the abuser to effectively do something about it.

Violence—domestic, private, or public is not a private affair. It affects us all terribly in ways that may last for generations to come. It not only demonizes the neighborhood but also the witnesses and victims who choose to do nothing thereby relinquishing their own authority and power. It causes people to live in fear of the abuser and of violence. It changes the feel and look of a community and the infrastructures are continuously reviewed and changed to protect victims and potential victims, and to accommodate abusers.

Thesaurus English (United States) defines victim:

Victim: *injured party (n); prey (n). A victim person is someone who is adversely affected by an action or circumstances; who is been tricked or exploited; who experiences misfortune and feels helpless to remedy it; who is hurt or killed by somebody or something.*

The purpose of abuse is to usurp all power and authority from the victims and the witnesses, and to make the Heavenly Creator's principles: commandments, laws, statutes, and judgments non effect. This usurpation of power is false and powerfully felt when allowed to go unrestrained.

When you acknowledge the need for true healing and growth, you will develop new skills in recognizing and exercising your authority and power to overcome such evil. You will be able to: more accurately discern evil behaviors of individuals you meet—especially those who want to be close to you; to powerfully exercise your rightful authority by quashing from the beginning any abusive behavior that are warning signs or actions against you and the ones you love and of other victims of abuse.

Such evil individuals when go unchecked and un-reprimanded will use cause and effects to rule over you in deep oppression

Chapter one

YOUR EGYPT

The name Egypt is used to describe a home where the inhabitants are abused and is not an environment where the only problem is misunderstanding easy to work through with much counsels and help. This type of Egypt is a place where evil is allowed to have complete control, especially, when done by a leader in the community, a lover, spouse, or caretaker of the home, and where children are involved.

Statistics regarding domestic violence worldwide corroborate the facts that no class, gender, color of people in society in the world is exempt from this evil. From the richest to the poorest, from the least to the most educated persons experience this pain. It is irrelevant what the economy is, as long as the oppressors believe they have the upper hand the situation will continue if not stopped.

Abusive environments are not good, is your Egypt in every way; a place where good is overcome by evil acts resulting in chronic abject poverty, and where great distresses are inflicted on you daily. It is a place where the enemy of our souls has taken full control and is angry because some of the inhabitants are not in agreement. As a result the home/environment has become a war zone and the unwilling participants become prisoners of war where they are mistreated daily.

Abusers created this place of haven for their own advantages at the expense of the oppressed and are not happy of the evil results of their actions which are quite the opposite of what they intended and know will not benefit them. They know every human being were created to be free for love and prosperity; and even being aware of this, it would appear quite impossible for their heart to be quieted because they are determined to abuse someone.

Their victims are unhappy and as a result rebellion may be numerous against them. They continue to exult in these horrible consequences; and due to the hardness of their hearts and the rapidly growing darkness within themselves, these results appear to them most advantageous and devastating to their victims. They rationalize it is best to keep the situation as is, continue hating you to keep their control over you, and if necessary with the aid of willing participants to help facilitate their objectives.

All forms of abuse are direct attacks from the enemy of our souls. No one is strong, educated, or sane enough to cope with this attack to mind, body, and soul. The enemy's goal is to kill your joy and harmony, your connection to our Heavenly Creator, and your rightful authority over all things, destroy your spirit and relationships, and in the end you must die.

Abuse used in this context of writing is to indicate the existence of great distresses of abuse, and is very clear that the human soul was not created for these kinds of distresses to be heaped on you. This may not apply to all readers and I hope not, but the fact remains there are people suffering this evil today mainly because of false beliefs.

HOW THEY TRY TO CONTROL YOU

The abuser may create mental, spiritual, psychological, physical, and financial obstacles to prevent and keep you from moving forward into areas where you can get what you need to continue to improve yourself. Abusers will always want to keep you *in your place* where they can control you—to lead you to what it is they want you to have, what you think you may have, and nothing more. They have created an environment where they perceived they are in total control with the intent to destroy you and it simultaneously.

A futile attempt to break the will of individuals to be forced to, or make automaton responses to the abuser's every whim is not such a pleasant sight as they envisioned, or believed would be successful. At first it may seem exciting that such a response can be facilitated from the victims. However, the creativity and ingenuity of affection displayed are lacking and does not appear authentic anymore.

These acts of expressions from victims will decrease until they cease completely as each acts of abuse are inflicted on them. When avenues for freedom to love and prosperity are blocked or threatened, and a way out is shown, the human soul must cry out and must not stop until it is free to bloom in the sunshine of love and prosperity.

In your Egypt you may have tried to reach out to people but none appear could be trusted, so for a while you dare not tell for fear of increased abuse. Your soul cries out day and night for deliverance from the possible causes of such evil behavior to cease and for improvement to be strong again. It could be drug- or alcohol-related issues, adultery, ill health, etc.

These are some examples of abuse you may experience:

Safety is critical to your well-being while in this place, but cannot be guaranteed. You are always on the alert, anxious, fearful, and as a result your physical health suffers. Your children are vulnerable and you may fear even more for their safety, which is paramount.

Isolation is the final stage to be mastered against victims of abuse, to have full control. They may devise plans to prevent you in communicating your needs and block your avenues for prosperity which may benefit them as well.

We were always very fortunate to live in areas where we met new friends who helped us in our times of disparities. Our safety is very important.

***Physical* abuse,** is another way of controlling you; designed to dehumanize, disable, and kill you, and as a result you will not be able to fight back. Harming you this way is attempted murder because the intent is to kill you. It is not an expression of love from the abuser as many victims may believe, and is self-sacrifice as you are giving up your physical safety to another who does not love you, and have no love for him/herself.

Financially, it may seem hopeless because you and your spouse together may earn more income than your neighbor, and may have least expenses, but unable to meet your family's basic financial needs. Your spouse's need to control the finances is not the same as controlling you financially.

To control the finances of the home is to meet all the needs of the family, and there is available emergency funding. To control you financially is to meet all the needs of the family but you will have no access to any reserve for your own personal needs; or to use up all his/her own finances for frivolous things which compel you to carry all the financial burdens of the family. As a result some very basic and emergency family needs cannot be met. These needs could be health, clothing, education, food, transportation, recreation, home improvements, insurances, etc.

This financial control may come through joint accounts. One spouse will see the other trying to save for a rainy day, and attempt to or succeed in draining the account very rapidly preventing all family needs to be met. The financial results can be devastating.

The inability to meet your own basic needs and that of the family can be very devastating and it shows. Your whole being seemed transformed or disfigured by the emotional pain associated with this great distress hard to deal with. Basically when you have financial difficulties it requires two finances working together and a meeting of the minds working it out calmly to meet the needs of the family and to make future plans for success.

Emotionally, this is not a safe environment because you cannot discuss with your spouse all this injustice that ails you and the family. The constant hostile behavior toward you tells you in no uncertain terms discussion is not allowed, you have no access to what is happening nor the freedom to understand and react to get help to equalize the situation and reason for justice and solutions. You are caused to feel displaced, deprived, and not safe. Any attempt may lead to verbal abuse and possibly physical abuse—a no win situation because all communications are blocked.

***Mental/psychological* abuse** is designed to shut you down always; to nullify your brain and eliminate your capacity to think, reason, react in healthy ways. Mental abuse is one of the first tools of offenses used against an intended victim with the intent to frighten him/her into submission and subjugation to be in most malleable state to be abused. At the beginning of this assault if the intended victims do not take a strong stand against it, then they are pulled into the self-centeredness the abuser has chosen to function in.

Mental abuse will cause you to question your own capacity to think logically and rationally, to decipher the difference between right and wrong, to question your true self-worth and identity created by the Heavenly Creator. It exist in abusive words, lack of right communications, deliberate misinterpretations and declassifications of victims' identity, and rightful expressions of love lacking in the abuser.

Mental abuse may not be accompanied by physical abuse. The abuser may feel he/she is more superior, more intelligent than the victim, and rationalize for the victim that to be loved or accepted by them, they must speak, act, and be successful like them; but lack the love necessary to help achieve all this. If the intended victim takes a stand against such unrealistic demands, they are declassified as immature, childish, stupid, and in other demeaning ways.

Mental abusers are not healthy in most ways. They may recognize that but chose not to seek professional help. They may abuse as a result of alcohol or substance abuse, other harmful habits, wrong advices, or other reasons.

Mental abusers choose their intended victims they think they can control. They may seek after those who they think have certain character traits they perceive are inferior to them, not necessarily identify with, but to easily control. They are not always correct in their assumptions, most times are, but not always. They do not have a desire to love their intended victim but will bear their time sometimes patiently until they are successful in gaining the trust of their intended victim, if not they move onto another.

Mental abuse occurs in all levels of relationships; in the workplace with coworkers, in friendships, in religious organizations, in homes, socially, locally, and internationally.

When mental abuse is inflicted on children, it is most devastating, designed to cause the children to not ever live to know their potentials.

It is designed against them at the beginning of the formative years to deprogram and rewire their neurological pathways, blocking the healthy release of healthy hormones responsible for healthy and timely development. As a result they do not know peace, cannot identify with it, their immune system will be affected and they suffer many series of illnesses. Their inability to perceive correct love is altered, because they not feel safe. It beats down the children's self-worth during their growth stages, causes their purposes in life to be derailed as they are frustrated to the maximum, causes much mental illnesses in life, and possibly death.

Mental abuse is designed against them to cut off their true identity and connection with the Creator, and to cut off their future generations.

Mental abuse is spiritual attack and in the literal sense a major tool designed by the hater of our souls who attempts to block our capacity to be connected to our Heavenly Creator. By connecting to Him we are taught our true identity in Him, our self-worth develop in healthy ways, improvements in all areas of our life, we are able to identify our true potentials and develop abilities to walk in them, and to contribute to society in healthy ways. Mental abuse is designed to derail you from this healthy life to reverse all these, and the repercussions are felt throughout society.

Spiritually, the children feel disconnected from the Heavenly Creator by whom they were told to love their parents. Been disconnected emotionally is to be disconnected spiritually. When a child is purely loved by someone, anyone, that child's emotions feed their spiritual health and the child feel and know they belong to someone who cares. This experience of been nurtured rightly allows the child's brain to experience some relief for times when they are experiencing normal stress, however short it may be. In an abusive environment, this emotional nurturing is not preparation or strength to cope with long-term abuse, because it is totally against the human nature, DNA, and rightful development of the pattern of neurological pathways to live and cope with distress as a result of long-term abuse been inflicted on them.

A distressful situation is when you have passed your point of endurance and continued to be heaped on emotional and physical pain.

Webster's Dictionary defines:

Distress *n. severe trouble, mental pain; pressure, hunger or fatigue or want; extreme pain, physical; misfortune; extreme poverty; (v.t.). To cause pain or anguish to; to harass, cause suffering.*

Physical, financial, psychological, emotional, and spiritual pain is caused by extreme situations constantly heaped on you with no room for thought, healing, and restoration. To the abuser it is the result that matters; to control situations and people to such severe degree that they are rendered or declared persons of low self-worth or disabled, finally in a situation where to the abuser the victims seem malleable. The intent of the abuser is not only to control the victims, but to control situations to cause the victims to react in predictable or degrees of manner to prove to the witnesses they are correct in their cruel actions.

The family's basic needs are not met; for medicine, food, clothing, education, recreation, transportation for work and school. As a result, when illnesses occur in the family they are forced to endure without medication for extended periods of time, contributing to further emotional and physical pain for cycles of time. This can cause other repercussions: diseases of the body, mental health suffers as the body is forced to endure such physical pain, hunger, and nakedness for extended periods of time.

Nakedness is not walking around without clothes on. It is the inability to clothe oneself and or others in your care adequately and appropriately. Not fashion shows, or collecting tons of clothes, but adequately and appropriately. Having enough of these clothing for activities and daily living is important for the body and mind.

Hunger is also the lack of good quality food. Adequate amounts of proper nutrition are an absolute necessity for balanced health. Food must be available constantly which includes storing enough food in freezers and dry foods for those times when you know you will need them and for balanced diet. You do not need a room full but it is important to have stored up nutritious foods. Medication is involved here to be available at the appropriate times and enough to ensure improved health.

SOME EFFECTS OF ABUSE

You may think as an adult you can cope with all this darkness—sometimes, maybe, but what of the children's state of mind. How do they see this darkness? At what cost we subject them to this and for how long? Is our silence and inactions worth their suffering? They too feel acutely the intense results of this darkness mainly because they are helpless to avoid it and they lack the skills to cope or move away from it.

To them it is a fearful situation. They are fearful of never been loved by the abuser, and perhaps the fear of or the reality of been rejected by the abused parent. They see their situation and determine that they are unable to endure it. They have endured beyond what they should be enduring and life can tragically go the wrong way for them, easily. They can either die under the heavy burden of oppression; become mentally ill; or they may look back to the only security they have—the abusive parent, and identify with the abuser in every desperate attempt to let that parent hear that they love them hoping the abuse will stop. They will simply and unwillingly comply with every whim and command as if to say—"As long as you do not hurt me. I will even blame the other parent and other siblings as long as you stop the abuse and make me safe." An internal fury of emotional hell the child is forced to endure, and a false sense of security created for the child.

Psychologists, medical professionals, and scientists are proving now that bipolar and schizophrenia in most cases in young adults can be traced back to long-term exposure to intensive abusive home environment.

The adult victim must constantly reassure the children that they are loved by their Heavenly Father, family, and friends, and are not responsible for the abusive parent's behavior. Against the controlling odds of the oppressors/abusers creating circumstances to cause the children to be alone with them, the other parent must make every attempt to assure the children's safety. Discernment is paramount in this case, yet, the situations are not always avoidable. Your nerves will always be on overdrive to secure their safety and of yourself.

To oppress someone is to break the will of an individual, to cause them to lose their own autonomy and balance, their own self, the great potential for success, ability to love, dance, and laugh, and make others happy by their own contribution to society in their own way. This is what happens to prisoners of war in this kind of war.

Internet source: The rightful expression of love.

http://ghalibana.blogspot.ca/2011/01/my-notes-art-of-loving-by-erich-fromm.htm

- *In Fromm's book, The Art of Loving (Harper, New York 1957; London Allen.) Love is an art. As it is an art, it needs knowledge and effort for its nourishment.*
- *The problem of love is not primarily the problem of being loved, but the problem of loving, of one's capacity to love. Love is an effort to overcome human separateness.*
- *Love is an act of giving—giving of ourselves, not from ourselves. *Basic elements of love: care, responsibility, respect, and knowledge.*[1]

You are realizing that the right interpretation and expressing of true love is by no means a stretch of the imagination. It is reality and does exist, obviously not in the abusive environment. Right love should elevate you to greater accomplishments than what you can imagine, if only in the attempt you should be free to attempt. It is a spiritual force, the Father's holy presence and His call to His grace that propels you to reach Him, eager to learn each day how to love in His context of pure love.

The scanty expression of affection displayed in the abusive home does not reflect that nor of the abusers' love for themselves. Indeed, it expresses hatred for something that does inhibit the abusers' capacity to love purely. Because love is inhibited in your environment, you are not safe. You may have tried to express love in the hopes that the abuser will stop, but expressing love in fear is not true love. It is indeed self-sacrifice. You are compromising all self-worth to get nothing in return.

You are held in a form of stasis where no growth is allowed and the darkness is growing deeper each day as you are forced to live in fear.

This darkness is also known as anxiety, and is not welcome in our lives due to its crippling affects.

Chronic Toxic Stress in Young Children and Executive Functioning

Internet Source: **http://www.heinz.org/grants_spotlight_entry.aspx?entry=1124**

This video of Office of Child Development Co-director Robert McCall introduces the concept of toxic chronic stress and what it means for children in adverse environments. Are there ways to mitigate the stress?

Typically, when a person is stressed (nervous or scared), their body produces an automatic response that serves either a flight or fight response. Under normal circumstances, this automatic response is a helpful reaction that keeps us safe from danger. However, if that person experiences chronic stress and anxiety on a daily basis, their body's involuntary response to that stress starts to negatively affect their health. This is especially true for young children. If a child endures anxiety-inducing situations on a regular basis, the stress typically begins to hinder the child's brain development as well as his/her emotional, and physical development. These instances of harmful, prolonged anxiety and tension in a child's life are referred to as chronic toxic stress.

Prolonged anxiety can be fatal, a slow killer as cancer. I often wondered how long we had to live while living in the abusive home. Every hour of the day there was reason to fret about something. It was nonstop: the unnecessary bills, the abusive words, the financial oppression, and fear of abusive actions toward us. I was constantly sick due to fear and constantly visiting my doctor. He had taken several tests and found nothing because he was not looking for more than the basics. The entire body suffered intense pain and was warped because of this great anxiety.

Doctors are proving that the body does suffer real pain and distortions and diseases due to prolonged anxieties. The spine in particular where all the nerves are connected reacts to distresses resulting in distortion of the spine. The nerves express pain in various areas of the body that is enduring great abuse. Anemia is also associated with living in an abusive environment.

You know the quality of life you want to live and this is not it. There are the unnecessary conflicts, disrespect, you have been talked down to, and physically abused. It can be very disgraceful at times especially, when the behavior excels to public grandstanding. These are the abject poverty and great distress you endured daily. When you are in this place there appear no way out. At times it seemed the situation was not all that bad, but that sense of security was only temporary.

The quality of living that everyone should pursue is not the life filled with material wealth and misery. Wealth is important to obtain the basic necessity of life to have comfort and the quality of life you want. Good health is an absolute necessity to help maintain a good quality of life.

It includes having a place where you call home—rent or owned to be a safe haven to return from the stress of the outside (work, violence, bad weather, traffic, mean people, etc.). It is a place you can rush to get home, to breathe that sigh of relief, pray, read a good book, cuddle with your children, spouse, and laugh together. It is a place where your children are safe to grow in dignity, love, wisdom, and be restored and refreshed in every way. You are free to walk in dignity, respect, and joy knowing you can face each day with a smile and overcome any obstacles of life because you have that security of home and safe relationships to include family and friends over to bond together with dinners, laughter, worship, etc. You are free to laugh at your own mistakes and endure your own financial and emotional losses, and to decorate sensibly and enjoy it. None of these are to be replaced by anyone.

In your Egypt, every inch of possibility for happiness in your own environment has been explored. For years you have worked hard for hope of succeeding in seeing your marriage succeed. You may have prayed long hours for deliverance. It is not only of your own prayers you will receive deliverance, you also need the prayers of others outside your abusive environment and of the other victims inside your home. It is important that this happens and the victims know that they are not forgotten, people care long-lasting for them, and they will not go it alone. The friendships develop during this time are bonds that continue long after the escape from the abusive home. When the victims pray and support each other for deliverance, there is strength to continue, plan, and help keep their sanity, especially with children.

Once I was in desperate need of something and thought if I told my son about it, he may become stressed. As a mother I believed it was only my responsibility to pray about it. Well, I was very wrong. I decided to tell him about it, explained the situation in the simplest way for him at that extremely young age could understand, and he understood. He prayed with me, and his prayers were more heartfelt than mine. I was strengthened by the purity of faith of a little child and our prayer was answered in a very short time.

We continued to pray together about most things today. This is very important, because children who bond together with family or parent, suffering or not stay bonded with us. As they get older they will go through their normal stages of growth but they will be much calmer. They will not grow utterly selfish but can easily empathize with others.

Each attempt to leave the abusive environment has been obscured by the constant pain been inflicted on you. Because of the prolonged endurance, it seems your nerves have been reprogrammed to feel nothing but pain. Your facial expression expresses pain constantly and your body has lost its good posture. Your posture reshaping is a clear indication of the oppressive power of gravity and weight of abuse. Your soul is constantly grieved because you cannot love or encourage enough to receive back any words of kindness to relieve the soul. Because of the non return of encouragement receiving only abusive words and actions, you are forced to hate everything about the one you vowed to love. The rare moments of affection expressed cannot be seen as promise of love to endure, because they are immediately afterward darkened by words of hostility and hate. This dangerous game of cat and mouse, and Russian roulette with your well-being will cause you to be afraid to love back because there is no emotional safety.

While in that marriage, most times I was scared to bring up a topic however encouraging or funny it may be. Clear words of encouragement were quickly returned by avalanches of insults. It numb the nerves to even try to explain to an individual like that what words of encouragements were meant to be. You will find out quickly you are on a suicide mission—a self-destructive path to help an abusive partner feel good. It is not in them to properly interpret good words and as a result you lack the freedom to purely love that individual because their brain is wired wrong.

Chapter two

HOW DID YOU GET THERE?

Yes, evil does exist everywhere, and most times unavoidable. It can be very easy to say, *"It really does not matter how you have entered your abusive life. What really matters is what you do about you."* That in some situations may be true, especially the latter. But it really does matter how we got there—in the abusive life. If we claim it does not matter, then we are totally dismissing our full responsibilities to learn from our past, grow in the process of learning, and mature appropriately.

I will address two of the many main reasons why we entered such an awful life of abuse.

1. *Genesis 15:16 . . . The sins of the Amorites has not yet reached its full measure.*
2. *Lack of right values in family: families—communities and cohesiveness.*

These are two of the main classic examples that truly illustrates the main reasons good and innocent people suffer all forms of abuses at the hands of abusers, and why sometimes we are compelled to change routes in our lives or take the long and expensive road to achieve later what could have been achieved earlier, safer, and most cost effective in a shorter time where we were.

1. To relocate as a result of someone else's *mistreatment toward you*, may give you the chance for survival and become stronger in time, as it did for the multitude of slaves living in Canaan and others who were mistreated by the Amorites. This relocation would strongly indicate that they may have been in imminent danger remaining

there in their own countries been constantly victimized by a nation stronger than themselves; threatening to eliminate their chance for real growth and survival. Then to relocate to another place and to be abused later may appear paradoxical when asked the question "Why trade one for another?" Yet the above verse does sound like an oxymoron statement, but true in its entirety.

Many reasons people left their countries, towns, and communities:

A. Intense persecution (political or religious) which threatens survival and growth.
B. Relocation from home town because neighbors are attempting to be a lynch mob against them.
C. To escape an abusive spouse or lover.
D. To escape abusive parents and/or siblings
E. Opportunities for employment and education are available elsewhere.

Evil does exist everywhere, though in various degrees and most times unavoidable. When we entered our relationship all may have appeared not bad at first, especially if our safety was not immediately greatly compromised. We had great expectations, hopes, and dreams to be realized. Gradually or overnight the scene began to change to indicate our safety will be greatly compromised and all our hopes, dreams, and expectations will either be on hold temporarily or be quashed permanently.

Why you are required to leave is because the evil actions of the abuser had compromised your safety, threatening to, and or stunting your growth. To continue living in that abusive environment your growth will be frustrated to the level of your intense anger due to the abject poverty you are enduring.

To reach the full measure of evil does indicate; as far as the abusers can or will in the time frame of you living with them, or is involved in their life emotionally and or physically and are in great danger with them. Yet this does not mean their entire full measure is complete. When their full measure is complete it means that the abusers have reached the farthest, or the lowest they possibly can to be evil to the maximum to all by their surrendering of self to evil thoughts, and evil intents (actions and motives), and to evil influences which enables them to harm you and greatly compromised your safety. At this point, the abuser has become a great danger to themselves and to society at large, and you are caught in the cross fire.

For you to reach your full potential or have the opportunity to attempt you need safety, and because your safety cannot be guaranteed in the abusive home, you must leave to a safe place far from the abuser. It will take powerful authorities in society to control them, not the excessive nurturing and your displaced sympathies, however well intended which may have amplified your risks from the beginning when trying to change the beast to a pussycat or by giving them levels of respect they did not deserve.

The multitude of slaves left their homeland because they had no food and their safety was greatly compromised, which greatly affected their chances to provide for themselves. It is not because Egypt was a perfect place, but the degree and the intensity of evil at that time of their relocation were far less. This they were able to endure which gave them a chance for survival and education and to live good quality lives—for a while.

With deep sorrow the Heavenly Father had warned them not to settle there. He knew the full measure of evil that will overcome Egypt and planned to deliver them.

2. ***Lack of right values in family: families—communities and cohesiveness.***

    - They *failed to be a cohesive family and family-communities.* They did not work together to improve their lives and fighting against each other which caused the surrounding nations to oppress them more.

In an intimate relationship this situation can be equally *intense* and we may have often asked why He had not warned or stopped us from entering such an awful life. He did try but because He did not shout it out at us we did not take heed. He did allow us to see the displaced dispositions that were indicators of future problems. Also through our own conscience we had hints and people warning us. If He had shouted it out we would say He is harsh and does not care in the same way we react to others who tried to warn us. He hurt because we did not take the time to get help.

Although the great multitude of slaves entered Egypt for food and chance for survival, most returned to their homeland when their land was restored. However, the remaining of the multitude of slaves who arrived for the same purpose remained there for more growth and had appeared to have escaped the "*dry valleys*" of their beloved home.

They escaped one "*dry valley*" for another. Their first was their own country due to famine and persecution. Their second was Egypt, although prosperous and green, it became a prison for them.

An abusive home/environment/relationship is also a "*dry valley,*" an area of abject poverty where dreams and visions of successes can never be realized. Many times we entered those "*dry valleys*" for the simple fact that we did not put great value on our own quality of life and instead chose partners whose quality of life is inappropriate and substandard to ours. Had we placed great quality on our own lives we would be better able to discern these *"dry valleys"* and their *"clouds without rain,"* and avoid them at all cost.

"Clouds without rain" are also *"dry valleys"*—areas of abject poverty and dreams only promised but the visions cannot be attempted to be realized. These prospective lovers may try to deceive you with promises they know they neither have the skills nor the desire to want to help you to be happy. They are objects of abject poverty.

Abject poverty is not always limited to financial poverty, but the absence of the desire of dreams and visions that need to be explored and to be fulfilled with the acceptance of failures and successes. However, the freedom to attempt must always be available and nurtured.

Lack of right values and its cohesiveness in family can cause people to settle into relationships which are ill compatible for them.

To be happy in marriage, single individuals must first be healed of all their past and current distresses, and be whole before entering intimate relationship. If not, they will never find happiness in a marriage. They will always be looking for that something or someone to fill that void in their lives which can cause them to enter a marriage with the wrong person and wrong expectations while disregarding obvious ill compatibilities.

Being single is neither accepted as normal or healthy status, and as a result many are succumbing to pressures from society, friends, family, and some religious communities to marry/remarry. Sure some want you to be happy, but many do not. Yet, while been pressured, stigmatized, and falsely accused of carnal sins they are not counseled, coached nor helped by those individuals in finding a mate. Neither are the potential mates been screened to benefit anyone and maintaining healthy relationships with others in their communities.

A. ***Lack of family involvement***. Couples cannot be everything to each other and they need the support of community and family members for belonging, friendship, and support to have a strong marriage. Unfortunately, many family members avoid been involved in their family circle saying, "It's not my business what they do, they are adults, they must ask for help if they want it. They will call me meddling or harassing them." Families must intervene, if even for the sake of the children.

To be isolated from community and families and in an abusive relationship is not good. It can cause the abusive spouse to have the upper hand in abusing the other.

Family involvement is important on a regular basis. They will be able to help guard the home from the onslaught of the enemy. In many cultures this support is available and marriages are strengthened.

Even though there do exist abusive spouses, isolation is not as successful against the victims when families are close. In our western cultures, too many families are isolated not only in distance but in emotions. Even though distance does play a part, emotionally if they are connected, it will not prevent the families to be close and support each other. Strong families inspire others to be strong. They spend time together to nurture and teach each other. This is the active loving our children need to see for safety and healthy growth.

B. ***Anger, lack of forgiveness, and unkindness*** toward each other play a huge role in isolation of families. Lack of forgiveness to our own spouse and children, own families, extended families and friends contribute in great part to an abusive environment. Extended families are caused to feel they are not welcome or belong to each other. If even the extended families were to look within themselves and are able to see their roles are extremely important to the new family, these feelings of anger, lack of forgiveness, and unkindness would be kept to a minimum and have no influence to destroy their bond.

C. ***Families—not extending love to children***. Children in the family need the love and support of extended families and friends. They need to see that active love and attention from them. We need to reach out to children of each family who are connected to us not only by blood and marriage, but also by friendships formed and bonded. When we isolate our children from families and our friends who are good and some not so good, we are saying to our children "You are not worth love." "We do not care for you." When they grow in this way, all their lives they are hurting deeply in the worst ways. Our children need to know that even if the abusive parent does not care about them, that there exist people in our immediate circle and beyond whom they can form bonds with and run to if need be.

Trying to raise them by ourselves without community and family intervention good or bad when they grow into early adult years, some will definitely rebel, and some in the worst ways. They rebel because they did not experience that love from family and family friends. They have been taught to raise themselves, live on their own, live for themselves, and not to value themselves or family. This is too painful, and because they have not experienced this kind of love, they may not know it. Some will crave it as they become adults and do their best to prevent this from happening to them and their children. Some will hurt too deeply and become angry, and will see these kinds of isolation as the only way to live and raise their children.

They will grow to see other young adults who are loved by their families and friends become successful in something, and will wonder why they at the same age cannot succeed in something too. They start to mourn deeply the lack of attention from family members who never invested interest in them in anyway, the isolation caused by their parents, rejection from religious circles, and teachers, which caused them to express hurt in numerous ways cannot be comprehended by the community in large. It is very real. This kind of isolation is happening more frequently as parents want to be *all* to their children. It is an impossible mission to venture on.

Psychology—*Themes and Variation*, 6th edition by Wayne Weiten, 2004. Myers (1992) offers some interesting conjectures. Among other things, he discusses how *religion can give people a sense of purpose and meaning in their lives, help them accept their setbacks gracefully, connect them to a caring, supporting community, and comfort them by putting their ultimate mortality in perspective.*

It is important to belong to a religious community that includes your children in many ways. However, hatred toward children raised by one parent is increasing at an alarming rate in most religious communities. They do not care whether the parent died, child was conceived by violence, or was abused. This happens because they the leaders increasingly defiantly disregard the Heavenly Father's true principles in how to be kind to the fatherless and the widow and they bring Him down to their level. Why? They think He is just like them, and they are wrong. **Psalm 50:16–22**.

In healthy religious communities, children may be nurtured to some extent. However, their influence cannot supersede that of family and close friends who love them. In abusive religious community, you and your children may be victimized to the extent you allow them, to the extent they see how you treat each other, and in most part—to the extent of the already existing darkness in their soul. It is worst for your children when you mistreat them in their presence; this is how they will most likely be treated by others who witness it. This is not to dismiss the fact that children who are loved are not targeted by other people in society. It does happen. Bad things do happen to children who are well loved and whose minds are pure. But by treating each other good we will have the power to command respect from our communities for our family. When you mistreat your family, you will neither have the will power nor the desire to command respect or justice for your family. Families and communities who uphold these values are strong.

*E. **Remarry***. Even though it may be good to have another adult in your life to replace the missing parent, at times it is not good. Often times it is with good intentions a single parent may marry to have another adult around to help guide their children. This requires serious and intensive counseling because the safety of the child must come first. As we are well aware many children are abused by a stepparent. This is not a stepparent syndrome. It is plain evil that the adult allows to enter their soul and nurtured to injure children because they are not biologically connected and the biological parent is missing for whatever reasons; look at the child as representative of or is the other parent and becomes resentful and perceives the child as worthless.

When families are closely connected, single parents will not feel pressured in thinking they must remarry regardless of the ill dispositions of the mate in question to provide for their children. With the help of counselors, friends, family, community activities, religious circles, single parents can be successful in rightly raising their children to be successful.

When we do not love each other right, we are abusing each other. We are saying to each other "We are not worth loving." When partners stop valuing themselves, they will not value their children. Then they find themselves at war with each other and if not stopped will expand on those false values. It means the vicious cycle of abuse may continue and with each person or next generation. What will happen to the individuals they have allowed into their immediate lives expected to love and honor them?

Now you are in a marriage or companionship that causes you to fear, we were not all bad at first. You may have wondered at this point; where this behavior came from—so suddenly? It was quite clear that they did not appear "suddenly." There were hints all along to indicate that there will be serious problems later. However, they were dismissed hoping with love and time they will disappear. Yet we try to hold onto the good while the evil increases and soon forget the good as we are more exposed to increased evil on a daily basis. Trying to reason out the lesser of evils to verify why you should stay will not work.

You may have entered a union with someone whose temperament is ill compatible to yours and is questionable, hoping it can improve overtime with love and much effort. Yet overtime it increasingly becomes worse and out of control, becoming nothing but hard work rewarded with sorrow.

When a relationship becomes abusive or distressful it is not a workable relationship.

Chapter three

HOW OUR CREATOR SEES ABUSE?

He *sees abuse as a covering of violence for the abuser and the abused.*

When we become violent to each other this is what happens to us:

Malachi 2:16: *"'For the Lord God of Israel says that He hates divorce, For it covers one's garment with violence,' Says the Lord of hosts, 'Therefore take heed to your spirit that you do not deal treacherously.'"*
Amos 5:15: *"Hate evil, love good, establish justice in the gate."*

The abuser use abuse as a cloak of his/her religious beliefs, and to the abused it becomes an ugly, burdensome, and unclean covering.

The abused individual's spirit is also a covering of violence. It does not matter how nicely the individual dresses, their soul is communicating with your soul—something is wrong, they are suffering deeply. This kind of suffering is not the same as hunger, loneliness, tiredness, or temporary poverty. It is a garment of heaviness. They cannot dress nice enough to hide this type of covering. It is wreaked with violence and fear.

No evil to be allowed in our communities—religious and secular, the abusers are to be corrected of their evil behaviors and not be tolerated.

People are more intimately identified with religion. Religious communities play a great role in the family regardless of culture. It is a circle they crave for sense of belonging. It molds their character to function in their inner and outer circles—home, school, work, social, marriage, and even on an international level.

The definition of divorce is always limited to a legal procedure in marital situations. Yet the Father throughout the Bible described divorce as intense violence, abuse, a separation from Him and from what is good to what is bad. Example in Ezekiel 16, He described the nation of Israel's behavior as adulterous and treacherous.

He sees abuse as disloyalty; committing high treason against Him—a violation against His principles—commandments, laws, statutes, and judgments and against our loved one. His principles are set in place to govern His kingdom in heaven and on earth for harmonious living with each other in our daily lives.

He equates them to intent, motives, and actions. To decide to put away your spouse whether by violence or simply divorce is to have already separated yourself from that individual in heart and practice.

If you are uncertain of what an abuser looks like, He will show you because He does not want you to be hurt. Your instincts will correctly discern the evil in them regardless of their charming/ charismatic dispositions. If someone is not evil, you will feel at ease, safe, comfortable with that individual enough to work and talk with them as healthy human beings, and to have them as your neighbor or friend.

Where is the blessing for an abuser? I have witnessed from my childhood into adulthood abusers who behaved so powerfully in playing God, their lives come to nothing. These abusers are men who walk away from their pregnant girlfriends; girlfriends who abandoned their loving male partners; married spouses who commit adultery; mentally abusive to friends, family members, and their children.

They are insecure single individuals with low self-worth who are not healed and look for victims to portray onto their insecurities. They are coworkers/employers who are bullies, and may want to sexually abuse employees in and out of the work place. They are secular or religious leaders who do not care about you being abused and have the audacity to want you to run back to the abusive spouse. They are repulsed by your circumstances and take every opportunity to insult you. Some of such leaders are abusive to their own families and some also sexually interfere with our young children and adults in and outside their immediate communities. They do this because they take unto themselves false license to hurt others and assume no responsibility and accountability. They claim the biblical principles are done away with, they cannot be held accountable, so they think. So horrendous are these false beliefs that it does cause individuals, homes, and communities to be at risk.

You may not believe all this is abuse, but they are. It is emotional, physical, spiritual, and mental abuse as you will see the trails of grievous affects they have left behind. Some of these damages are irreparable and can be long-lasting especially if children are affected, or when they are encouraged by others to hate and mistreat you.

Some have claimed that these abusers are sincere and religious. It does not matter what great skills, education, or position in life they may have possessed, if they decided to abuse, it would appear the Father steps in and cuts off the covenant He made with them.

Others have even reasoned, "This abuser is a good and religious person. They attend worship every day of the week. Look they are leaders in the community. They are loved and adored by everyone and nothing bad will ever happen to them." Others have even argued that the unfaithful spouse is right in doing this because "maybe their spouses at home are not giving them enough love. You need to show more respect and stop talking evil about them." Can an abuser ever be satisfied? Well, think again. Does the Father care about their reputation? What does He say about abuse? Read all of Malachi chapter 2. Even though He was talking to the Israelite nation, He narrowed it down to family, present day family—traditional and modern.

Malachi 2:12-14: *"And this is the second thing you do: You cover the altar of the Lord with tears with weeping and crying; So He does not regard the offering anymore, Nor receive it with goodwill from your hands. Yet you say, 'For what reason?' Because the Lord has been witness between you and the wife of your youth, with whom you have dealt treacherously. Yet she is your companion."*

When the abuser feels punishment for their crimes against their family, they start to cry asking why He is allowing this to happen. They do not prosper as He promised them because he or she dealt treacherously with another.

He is saying "Do not call on me in your self-righteous attitude expecting me to give you what you want, while at the same time you are abusing your neighbor, coworker, mother, father, girlfriend, boyfriend, spouse, and children who love you according to what I put in them in how to love you, and you are playing Russian roulette with their heart. Look your spouse is the one who cared for you day and night, make love to you and you treat your spouse as though he/she is garbage. Do you not think I see everything, including the intent of your heart?

It was very difficult for me to hear the prayers and complaining of the abusers. I was very repulsed by them and often wondered why they allowed themselves to get to this point in their lives. They simply refuse to acknowledge that they are not gods, only humans who need their Creator to guide them daily to live decent lives. They try to be god to their spouse and children insisting the whole world be centered on them.

People continue to argue that these abusers do not deserve punishment. "There is some good in them. After all they are good to me." Well, think again.

Malachi 2:17, *"You have wearied the Lord with your words; Yet, you say, 'In what way have we wearied Him?' In that you say 'Everyone who does evil is good in the sight of the Lord, and He delights in them,' or, 'Where is the God of Justice?'"*

He is saying here, why are you complaining that the person been punished is good, not deserving of punishment. They must choose between good and evil and take responsibility for their wrong actions. He does not and cannot take delight in seeing others abusing others. It hurts Him and He will punish the abusers. Does that mean He is not just? If He does not punish the wicked how can the victims be safe? How can others learn that it is not acceptable? This gradual degradation of pure values if not corrected from the beginning will become a norm in our communities and our lives.

Chapter four

HOW OUR CREATOR FEEL ABOUT ABUSE?

The heart of our Creator was filled with sadness when He told Abram in Canaan, many years before, of what will happen to his descendants in Egypt.

Genesis 15: 12-16. 12*: As the sun was setting Abram fell into a deep sleep, and a thick and dreadful darkness came over him, 12: Then the Lord said to him, "Know for certain that your descendants will be strangers in a country not their own, and will be enslaved and mistreated four hundred years, 14: But I will punish the nation they serve as slaves, and afterward they will come out with great possessions. 16: In the fourth generation, your descendants will come back here, for the sins of the Amorites has not yet been fulfilled."*

This place He referred to was Egypt. Initially, a place where good once existed; Joseph an Israelite, son of Jacob, sold by his brothers (Genesis 37), suffered many hardships there (Genesis 37–40), and eventually became vice president in Egypt. Under his rule everyone was treated well.

A great famine came, which affected Egypt and many surrounding nations, and because Egypt was prepared for the famine, they came there to be fed. Egypt appeared to them more prosperous than their own countries, and after the famine ended and their land restored, many returned while many remained in Egypt. Joseph died and the new leaders forgot his kindness to all. These new leaders were cruel in heart and did not follow Joseph's example of leadership.

The Creator had warned them not to settle there for anything and knew they would not be treated well there. He knew the darkness looming over Egypt, and saw in full details every character, every evil dispositions, and wrong values developing into evil results. He knew how the experience of been brutally enslaved would affect them, and wanted to spare them from such great distresses. They would not be free to worship Him, nor prosper as they should, and in the future their safety would be greatly compromised.

In His great love and compassion He saw and felt in advance their horrors and was gentle to Abram by putting him to sleep while telling him the horrible news. In the telling of this horrific news there was no joy in the anticipation of its fulfillment.

Two Bible translations say it well. **Genesis 15:12:**

New International Version: *As the sun was setting, Abram fell into a deep sleep, and a thick and dreadful darkness came over him.*

The New English Bible: *Then as the sun was going down, a trance came over Abram and great fear came over him.*

Webster's Dictionary defines:

Fear: *n.-dread, alarm, unpleasant emotion caused by coming evil or danger; v.t. regard with fear, revere, hesitate, shrink from*

Darkness: *n.-mysterious, wicked.*

Had the Bible only said: "As the sun was going down," or, "as the sun was setting darkness came over Abram and he fell into a deep sleep," then we can correctly assume it was only the regular darkness of night that gives the body the message for sleep, rest, and restoration.

The words *"dreadful darkness"* and *"fear,"* are synonymous with each other, amplified by the adjectives—*thick and great.* They are equivalent to *"horrible and frightening darkness."*

Webster's Dictionary defines:

***Horrible**: a.-horror, hideous, shocking*

***Horror**: n. terror, intense dislikes, or fears, something causing this.* This word *"horrible"* best describe, *"thick and dreadful darkness," "great fear"* that the Father felt and caused Abram to feel only some of it, expressing to Abram His true feelings and interpretation about abuse of any kind toward all His creations.

This horrible and frightening darkness that came over Abram can be found in some occasions in the Bible expressing only some of His description of all kinds of abuse. Not enough words in all the world's language combined can truly express the real hurt and pain of abuse. Had Abram been fully awake hearing this horrible news about his descendants' future demise in Egypt, he would not be able to understand or endure the full gravity of it.

1. ***Genesis 15:10–12***. This great darkness of the impending conflict to be inflicted on the multitude of slaves; great danger, slavery, abuse, death, abject poverty, and intense cruelties all this darkness emanated from the abusers creating despair for the victims.
2. ***Exodus 10:21***. The plague of darkness that occurred in Egypt: Pharaoh needed to get the message that he owned no one and has no rightful authority to abuse anyone. This thick awful darkness they felt, was what they had imposed on the slaves and their own citizens through their own evil actions. By forceful confinement they were blocking and preventing the slaves from connecting with their families and their Heavenly Creator to live healthy and

prosperous lives. The abusers now had a chance to feel the fear and violence they were compelling others to endure and it was most frightening for them.

3. ***Mark 14:33–36***. The intense pain, hurt, and sorrow inflicted on YaHoshua, the Messiah by the hand of the soldiers and the religious community was intense to the extreme. Now nailed and hung on a tree, been crucified, that "*horrible/great and thick darkness*" that encircled Him was the most horrific illustration of darkness representing evil the human eyes could ever see and the soul ever could comprehend, if at all what evil looks like and what abuse feels like. This horrible darkness was what appeared to be the entire demonic hosts of darkness from hell and all corners of the earth, covered the entire earth and especially concentrated on the spot He was nailed. They came to—

(A) ascertain that He, Yahoshua the Messiah was really the one they intended to eliminate from the beginning;
(B) to hold court—to determine to judge the Heavenly Father's character through Him;
(C) to cause the onlookers to doubt this sacrifice for the sins of all mankind now covered with complete darkness, could not be their Messiah the One to take away the sins of the world they were waiting for.

This scene of hell was so intense lasting for three hours, that no one could see anything before them; not even their own hands.

It was a foolish thing for the host of darkness to do as they, at their appointed time, unknown to them, showed up to be judged and condemned-hung on a tree. They came to meet their Creator, who is their judge, and executioner *and the being who* has all the complete attributes of the Heavenly Father with all authority and power. **Colossians 1:15–20**. He came for this purpose to bring down the powers of darkness and to judge and condemn them there, at the cross; the exact spot intended for their judgments, eliminating their powers of darkness over our souls (**2 Corinthians 5:17–19**).

When cried He had cried out, *"My God, My God, why hast thou forsaken me?"* He was not telling us His Father had forsaken Him. He was telling us in details what He had endured for all generations to know and ponder, already illustrated and prophesied in **Psalm 22**. In **John 19:30 He** cried out—*"It is finished."* He was illustrating to us in a most profound statement: the host of darkness is completely judged and condemned to die now waiting their final execution/destruction—when He return. His statement also greatly illustrated another reason for the presence of the host of darkness at His death.

(D) Unwittingly they fully and completely illustrated to the whole world and to all universes and to the holy angels what the great controversy between the Heavenly Father and Satan was really about: the fallen angel's intense hatred for His authority and love for His creations, and their mutiny against the Sovereign Creator.

Their intense focus on Him at the cross was a public declaration of their hatred for Him, to cause extreme agony of every kind to possibly sin and abandon His mission, to never be able to return to the Father, and leaving all creation vulnerable to them.

One can never fully describe nor ever understand what an entire host of demons spitting out abuse all at once sound or look like; but we can on a smaller scale in our own abusive home and environment what a few demons—propelling the abuser to abuse you sound and feel like compare to millions or trillions of host of darkness abusing you all at once is more than we can bear. Yet Yahoshua bore it all at once for everyone.

The Father had felt in horrors the increasing darkness that was to follow the slaves' escape and of which would engulf the entire world. They had escaped Egypt and other nations; but this darkness kept pursuing them. This darkness amply added to and aided the already existing present great darkness which appeared to be the whole hosts of darkness revealed on that day.

This dark presence on the day of Yahoshua's execution had increased continuously to this day. And for centuries after this darkness aided in the uprising of many nations and kingdoms' main goal is to continue inflicting injury on all humanity.

This great darkness expressed on that day also emanated from the souls of humans who not only took part in His execution but who also rejected Him. They had such great hatred for the Father that they reacted physiologically in most violent ways; so much that their entire being became complete conduits for this intense and continuous growing darkness.

Rarely has humans seen such physical darkness emanating from other human beings. We can sometimes see it eclipsed in the eyes only enough as the soul of that person tries to hide dark thoughts and feelings toward you; we would sense a spirit of danger or unrest from them; see the evil actions of others we call darkness due to its terrible results. More so today is visible that darkness or a darkness radiating/ covering of darkness from their body that covers them engulfing the soul emanating outward of their being indicating they have lost control of their spirit and are not connected to the true Creator.

To have fully emanating from the soul a physical darkness; to have fully given all self-restraint to evil thoughts, actions, intents, and to fully enforce all means and power to execute it outwardly.

This darkness does not develop overnight. It is a gradual letting go, or the denouncing of what is right to accept the wrong and the releasing of all self-restraint to what is dangerous regardless of reasoning and knowledge of causes and ill effects.

This darkness is sometimes quieted by reasoning but when all reasoning rejected and there are available avenues—opportunities for acceptance of the destructive then there remain no more restraint. "*Then all hell breaks loose,*" and we see more devastating results played out in our lives.

Chapter five

FAULTY VIEWS ON MARRIAGE

The main purpose of marriage is for the glory of the Creator: to create a special union of two individuals (man and woman) to restore the unity which was granted by Him in paradise; to allow each individual's space to grow to reach their highest potentials capable of reaching.

Why "for His glory"? He created you to be the best you were designed to be, that growth takes a lifetime and will extend into eternity. You were created to be His masterpiece and only He can complete it. Others who join you can only support you in that growth and will ultimately find joy in the process.

Then why so many faulty views on marriage exist? So many it is often times nauseating listening to many people trying to impose their own experiences and opinions as the only way to live. While some are not destructive most are not reliable sources. Very few really get to the heart of the matter, such as: true interpretation of the marriage vows; true respect for each other; communicating heart to heart; good/healthy financing; healthy individuality; treating others right; maintaining good health; and your purpose in life.

Many individuals shared with me their views on marriage. Tragically, less than 0.1 percent can give a straight answer. The other 99.9 percent could not think outside their own destructive dysfunctional marriage and often project their own lack in our marriage discussions.

Some are so oppressive while listening that I felt a heavy weight on my head, dark clouds overhead and warning signs telling me—*"Run for your life—far from marriage, and thank the Heavenly Father you are single. Hallelujah, praise the Lord. If that is really what marriage is all about, forget it. Who is married stay married, who is not, do not bother with it.*" But I do know better. The ultimate idealistic romantic in me says, "Too bad for these miserable so and so. They could apply a little more respect and compassion to their spouse and they would get so much love in return. What can be so hard about that?"

I do take note, however, and vow to never be like them with my future spouse. To apply any of their destructive advices would require me having split-brain surgery.

Although these individual lives may not be as tragic as my marriage went, there are sorrowful indications of dark undercurrents about to erupt soon if the other spouse does not remain strong. Within that 0.1 percent of straight answers, I have learned that not all men think in such oppressive ways, but I already knew that. Having the courage to discuss them before saying, "I do," can make a world of difference in strengthening your relationship and building a true foundation. You will know beforehand what will and will not work for your partnership, and that each individual requires certain freedom, space, and trust to truly grow as a healthy and successful individual.

These are some of the many faulty views revealed and adopted to our personal lives which are strong indicators singularly or combined may have precipitated an abusive situation:

1. *Lack of respect for the partner's individuality, true worth, uniqueness, and separateness. Both partners should respect each other to be the best husband, wife, and lover as created to be, and treat each other good.*

It is an imperative that a major characteristic of genuine love for each other is to recognize these distinctions between oneself and the other to be always maintained and preserved for mature marriage and growth.

When someone truly loves you they will respect and always encourage your uniqueness and separate individuality. If not, they will ultimately inflict unnecessary sufferings and cause much mental illness; not only onto their spouse, but also affecting others in their communities inflicting much suffering unto them. There are other reasons a partner tries to control the other.

(A) Not recognizing their own individuality, worth having one's own dislikes and likes, intellect, abilities, and skills to make choices for own self.

The spouse with wrong concepts of marriage and life values will think they must control the other to feel important. Example: Some spouse will demand the twenty-four hour whereabouts of the other spouse. Knowing where we are at most times is important for safety reasons. But this is extreme when anger is involved and the controlling spouse harasses and sometimes stalks the other, and insisting that before every thought to be acted on however minor and unique for that individual; what they must wear, eat, buy (minor items); cannot choose own career, simple decorations or clothing without discussion and permission of the other spouse must be discussed and agreed on by the inquiring spouse.

(B) The abusive spouse lacks the discipline of truly expressing love for one self and extending love to another. Basically, they are neurotics and out of control. This is narcissism. Most abusers in marriage believe that becoming one means a melting of the two minds into the other; because they connect physically and emotionally through sexual intercourse, the other spouse should be able to know what the other wants and expects at all times, even though the thoughts were not communicated. They are expected to always think the same, never disagree on anything, do only what the other wants, will do, and say.

This is giving up of one's own individuality and autonomy to another who wants to replace your own authority in your life. The abuser is expecting the victim to totally submit all of own self to them. While one loses to the other—own identity, self-worth, personality, and power to choose, the other wants to gain it all. This kind of behavior does neither allow any healthy confrontations nor freedom for creativity in problem solving and expressing love without the risk of marital failure.

2. *Traditional roles* in its efforts with most, good intentions, have tried to teach us about marriage, most times failed to help us identify and nurture our own individuality and separateness. For example: Some cultural traditions teach that a woman/wife must stay at home and care for the children, and not allow education. The former may be best suited for the health and safety of the children while very young, and the survival for that kind of arrangement to be successful. Even in modern families in modern societies, it may be agreed on by both spouses that for the best interest of the family survival-financially and for the best interest of the children to be well cared for at home.

   However, in many families where that arrangement is not necessary and the financial responsibility of the family is one spouse and is very limited that may be a strain and may cause unwarranted stress in the home. If the other spouse has the desire to help the family to be successful, that spouse should be given the freedom to explore healthy and creative ways in contributing to the family without too much neglect to the children. Whatever the educational achievements; both can contribute to a healthy family life.

In an abusive environment where all avenues for education are blocked and creativity for the generating of income to improve the health of the family and one's own health will only result in frustration for both spouses. Frustration for the victim who needs and craves the outlet for own expression, and intense frustration for the abuser who sees the degeneration of financial stability and the decline in the overall health and well-being of the family and surmised the stay-at-home spouse is to be blamed for all this mess. If they do not get help to work it out, it may escalate into other forms of abuse.

3. *Negative dependency.* Another dilemma that precipitates an unhealthy family life occurs when a healthy spouse holds the view that the other is totally responsible for their care will not contribute in establishing the home and not venture further while still draining the financial resources. The working spouse is always expected to do a full day's work and return home to do all the chores at home. These spouses will not keep the home clean and beautiful to be a pleasant retreat from stress. They have no skills and are not interested in developing any to make family life enjoyable. They choose to quit their jobs and educational pursuit, stay at home and venture no further. That could work only if there is an established work activity or work office at home that generates income to help sustain self and the family.

   This is addictive personality, always expecting the other to fill that void that no human possibly can. No one individual is totally responsible for the happiness of another. Such person is not concerned about the spiritual growth of the other, only interested in what they can get always, and never give back. They will not venture on their own to risk any growth and will not tolerate any unhappiness, suffering, and been alone in the process of growth.

They constantly demand compromising from the other spouse and—"If you love me you will do this or buy that for me." They fail to accept responsibilities and consequences of one's own actions. They use the word "love" as a cover up when life's ills and woes are present; afraid to grow beyond their own shadow without regard for the quality of the relationship. They lack wholeness and uses marriage to define them.

To prevent been too dependent, an individual must appreciate their own worth, intelligence, and assets, and work to develop them.

MARRIAGE—"AN INSTITUTION?"

Malachi 2:15: *(a) But did He not make them one, having a remnant of the spirit?*

Our Heavenly Father, our Creator never institutionalized marriage. He created marriage as a covenanted relationship between Himself, man and woman, and the community at large; a natural way of life to have the entire being one with His principles: commandments, laws, statues, and judgments.

We use the word institution because over the many centuries the words *covenant relationship* were lost to us and replaced by the word *institution* which only existed in the early 1400s.

Webster's Dictionary defines:

Institution. *N:—the act of instituting or establishing an established law, custom, or public occasion, an institute; an organized pattern of group behavior established and generally accepted as a fundamental part of a culture, such as slavery.*

If you belief that marriage is an institution, this may make perfect sense. But for those who desire the freedom for true growth and to have healthy lives and healthy communities, this definition applied to marriage can be very disturbing. Many questions should come to mind:

What established laws are used to define marriage as an institution? Should not the Father's already established principles: commandments, laws, statutes, and judgments make a marriage work? Are there separate laws for marriage different for daily living, and why replace them with culture and cultural behavior?

According to this definition of *institution* every culture has its own laws and customs which we know are often not established on our Creator's principles.

We transform marriage into an institution when we enter this relationship with wrong values, and our hearts darkened with our self-centered righteousness to use the vows as weapon of mass destruction against others: "You promised to obey me." "This is until death do us part." "You will not leave me. What happens in the home stays in the home. I rather see you dead than see you with another person or be successful by yourself. You promised to be with me for better or worse. I can do whatever I want to you, because you are my spouse," etc. These are wrong and evil views, but because the marriage vows are so full of ambiguity you are caused to feel you are at the mercy of a potential abuser, if, and when things go wrong. Abusers often do this to cause their victims to feel imprisoned because the vows sound so final and no reasoning is allowed.

Marriage is now called an *institution* because we say—His principles: commandments, laws, statutes, and judgments in how to live and treat each other do not make sense, do not apply to us, we need our own. And for the most part were not taught how. His principles are pushed aside to create our own rules and prefer to learn from trials and errors, which always proved to be very disheartening, extremely costly, and subjecting individuals to abuse and lifetime of suffering.

Marriage is also institutionalized when we impose wrong views on marriage. They insist for the survival of the family as one abuse must be tolerated to prove it can be endured, and the wedding vows can never be broken. The vows in this case become a powerful bulwark for the abuser and those who support such behavior by becoming spectator to your predicament.

While in the past abusive home, I was told reasoning was not allowed and the marriage vows were thrown in my face constantly causing me despair and feeling imprisoned. Some people we knew curtly informed me; "You made a vow and you must stick with them." "You should have realized before marriage what kind of person he was. Suck up princess, etc."

As a result of this thinking every marital home has become an institution with its own established separate laws: "This is a new home a new law. I am the boss here. I can do what I want." When things eventually go wrong no one has any authority to intervene. The abusers have no knowledge of their accountabilities or of their civil duty to others. Many people will attempt to correct them with the intent to protect the victims by showing the abusers the right way of living, are rebuffed by the abusers' harsh responses: "No one has the right to interfere, I am in charge here, and I can do what I want to my spouse. It's none of your business, stay out of it. This is between me and my spouse."

This is an attempt to nullify all of the Father's principles—commandments, laws, statutes, and judgments in establishing right and healthy living, because the abuser reasons—he/she is now a ruler—king of their own castle without boundaries. They now believe that our Creator thinks like them, because they joined themselves in marriage.

Those who are rebuffed are caused to question their own authority in such situations, because they do not know which of our Creator's principles are to be enforced, and the civil laws are sometimes quite ambiguous. They often times retreat in their efforts for fear of the victims' increased re-victimization in their absence. Unfortunately, the victims do not ask for help nor perceive that these interventions were open doors for their escape.

A classic example: Many years ago, I met a young woman, Timber, who confided in me that she was constantly abused by her husband who took the liberty in doing so because she did not have her immigrant landed status. I told her she can get help but she was too afraid.

One night while speaking to her on the phone about a job opening I heard her husband suddenly physically attacking her, and I heard her screams and cries of fear. I asked for her address and immediately put her on hold and called the police to her address. When I arrived, police officers were already there, encouraging her to leave and they will take her to a safe place where she could be helped, and he could be charged for assault, or be referred to an agency where he would be counseled to stop his cruel behavior.

The husband stepped out the door of the unit and asked me if I had called the police. I boldly answered yes. He was surprised of my boldness and stepped back inside his unit a bit more sober. The woman was on the floor in pain and was afraid to leave because she perceived she could not obtain her immigrant landed status without the abuser's help.

To the abusers the marriage vows are constantly in effect due to insecurity feeding the ego, resulting in power play and abuse. They use the vows as weapons of mass destruction, first in their hearts and eventually playing out in abusive acts toward their victims.

The marriage vows in the hands of people who revere their heavenly Creator are more than only a formality in getting married. They are aware of its true content and intent, and are determined to apply our Heavenly Father's principles—commandments, laws, statutes, and judgments in creating save and happy life. They know they are making a solemn promise to each other, and their communities at large to really love each other.

MISINTERPRETATION OF THE MARRIAGE VOWS

The first recorded expression of a marriage vow expressed by Adam to Eve when she was presented to him just before they became intimate as a couple can never be outdated by any current wedding vows.

Genesis 2:23–24 *"And Adam said: this is now bone of my bones and flesh of my flesh, she shall be called woman because she was taken out of man. Therefore shall a man leave his father and mother and be joined to his wife, and they shall become one flesh."*

Do you hear the excitement, commitment, and anticipation in his voice? The end of his loneliness! He is saying, "She is human like me, a part of me!" He sees her as a separate individual created by the Heavenly Father apart from himself to be with her, not to be lost in his individuality. He is also making it clear that his wife he will love and treat as his own body and no human or demonic influences will ever influence him against her, and nor will he instruct her to hurt others. He is promising to protect, nurture, respect, adore, love, and die for her. He acknowledged in a most powerful way that she belong with him.

The marriage vows between man, woman, were meant to be a covenanted agreement between them and the Heavenly Father, a great beginning for life together; a life of commitment, love, faithfulness, and truth that was intended to be in harmony with correct principles: commandments, laws, statutes, and judgments.

The real intent of the current vows we have today appears benign enough. However, due to gradual changes from *a covenanted relationship* to *an institution*, marriage vows now appear ambiguous and however unintended, give abusers license to abuse instead of responsibilities and accountabilities of own character.

Unfortunately, many enter marriage with grave doubts and fears about the spouse's ill dispositions and doubted how to correctly implement the wedding vows.

Abusers use them to create obstacles for their victims and because many were not taught the truth of their commitment, they use the vows as deadly weapons when ego takes over and as tools of offenses creating despair. For example:

(A) "We must obey." The abuser uses this to quash/eliminate your rights and responsibilities to reason on any point—wrong or right.
(B) "Until death do us part." Living with an abuser this is a death wish causing you to feel trapped in a marriage regardless of the abuses, until you are dead. You are literally signing a death contract on your life, worse if you decide to stay. For the abused and the abuser developing a martyrdom complex and lifestyle, which is basically a death wish, developed to prove to society that they the abused are better than the abuser or in a religious mentality a better *believer* than the abuser.
(C) "For better or for worse" was intended to be understood as: we work together patiently to live in harmony, to work out the finances together, cheer each other along to grow together in a safe and healthy relationship. For worse meant in sickness and in health. Sickness and good health happens to everyone, we often prefer good health. Bad things do happen: loss of jobs, bad situations outside our own control. In a healthy relationship this can work with much effort as there are frequent meetings of the minds and mutual love and respect for each other grows.

The marriage vows should be based on the Father's principles, commandments, laws, statutes, and judgments, truth, commitment, and true feelings before marriage that it would be natural and easier to love and nurture each other purely. They should be studied and analyzed and correctly implemented in our lives. If the marriage vows can be used as such deadly weapon, questions should be—then what were the true intents of the vows? There is absolutely nothing in His principles that can be used to abuse another. Were they pushed aside instead? If we were to base our marriage vows on these, there would be no excuse for abuse; because we would be held in the highest expectations of accountability and responsibility to Him, ourselves, all children, and to everyone in our communities.

If you are wary of how to live without ever becoming arrogant with each other, consider the following:

Malachi 2:15: *"But did He not make them one, having a remnant of the spirit? And why one? He seeks pure offsprings. Therefore take heed to your spirit and let none deal treacherously with the wife of his youth."*

Before marriage, make sure you are connected to the Almighty Sovereign Heavenly Father and Creator in every way to be healthy in body, mind, and soul. Your beliefs, values, and attitudes are to be based on His principles before marriage. He wants you to treat each other rightly—your homes and communities to be safe, your children and future generations to see through your behavior how to love their Creator, themselves, and others.

But what if your future spouse keeps saying they cannot help themselves in their bad behavior and claim that the marriage, or you, will help them to improve their behavior? Do you believe such nonsense? They will use the word "love" in the attempt to dismiss all ill behavior.

This I heard too often, some men who do not know the Heavenly Father, nor practicing their faith, say they want a *god-fearing woman to marry* and to hold their hand when they misbehave. Meaning: she is expected to know right from wrong, be humble always, accept and tolerate whatever abuses he dishes out. Their beliefs are: a god-fearing woman has no authority to fight back, and constantly be a shrink to them.

What does the Father say about all this?

Micah 6:8: *"He has shown you, O man what is good and what does the Lord requires of you, but to do justly, to love mercy, and to walk humbly with your God."*

This is telling you the Father had already put in each person's soul and DNA the ability to know the difference between right and wrong in making right decisions; what to expect from each other, how you to be treated, how to treat others, and what kind of character your friend to have before marriage. You are to know certain behavioral traits that give hints of future abusive behavior are not to be tolerated nor be dismissed.

This verse illustrates that couples are to be the light bearers/moral leaders, as they are in positions of authority in the home and in the community. Their conduct should be developed through the Creator's principles, giving good instructions to all, and respecting their family.

Some religious leaders impose the marriage vows as a romantic remedy for every wrongs inflicted on you. Yet when the abuses come they refuse to identify it as evil, because they have no knowledge of how to implement the Creator's principles in correcting these kinds of behavior. They kept insisting that the Father's principles have expired, with the intent in eliminating their ability and responsibility to discern right from wrong, and the abused are often reminded of the vows as pacifiers to their woes without correct counsels to relieve the heavy burdens placed on them.

Today, not many religious teachers teach against abuse and its grave results. Such leaders are extremely vague on the topic as though they have no authority on the matter, and wave it off as an extremely private matter that they think should not be spoken of.

They are afraid of such evil exposure and its "potential ill results" on their communities. I often wonder if they are abusers in their own families when they refuse to teach the plain truth about this kind of evil.

Unfortunately, for some women, they too have contributed greatly to their abusive life. For example:

(1) A wife's agreement with the husband to stay at home does not limit her contribution to a healthy family life. Financial dependency on the husband's income does not limit her creativity and wholeness in making the home clean, beautiful and a safe haven for the hard working spouse to be happy to return. Not accomplishing any of these result in negative dependency and is cruelty for the hardworking spouse who is ever burdened with all tasks—work and home.
(2) Preventing the husband from expressing his ideas and needs for the family to succeed. Often times such wives are so distressed in their own deception of creating a fantasy life they learned and adopted through false representation of correct marriages, demanding the husband provide it for them, and not cooperating with him or encouraging him to achieve it. Instead they often times oppress him and find ways to suppress all his visions to succeed that would eventually make her happy. This is hatred for her man she claimed to love and it may lead to abuse when frustration reached its paramount.
(3) Preventing him from healthy outlets for stress. Often times such insecure and oppressive wives will block their husband's healthy emotional and recreational outlets, preventing him from socializing with friends and family members and from expressing his creative interests in healthy and genuine ways that will help him cope with stress. While at the same time he is expected to love and idolize her as a queen.

(4) Uncleanness to body, mind, and soul. Such spouses lack the will and initiative to accept counseling and training to correct attitudes and develop skills to improve their lives. So locked in their own insecurities and unhealthy minds they often times will target others in their communities who they wrongly perceived to be a threat to them by inciting violence in others to think evil of them and hurt them especially. Their mind is not healthy and will often treat others with indifference. They are lacking skills necessary to help create healthy community cohesiveness, and are pacified by the cruelties imposed on others through their spouse as proof of love. They are not concerned for their spouse's reputation and safety in the community, nor of the victims'. Some spouses know the evil dispositions of their abusive spouse but will constantly defend them against their victims. They are so visible in their own darkness they do not perceive it themselves believing they are cunning in hiding it through their scanty rays of affections toward the victims, but evident to others and their victims.

Some spouses knew of their spouse's ill disposition and low self esteem and anger to attack others who correct them; will not stand against such behaviour, but rather support his behaviour by inciting violence against his victims.

All these are devastating especially for a male simply that: his integrity, self-worth, character, great potential for income, and success are been blocked. It is encoded in his DNA, and the commandments for him to be the lover, protector, defender, encourager, and the moral leader of the home and the community. He needs support from family members, community, and friends to accomplish all these in a timely and graceful manner. He cannot do it all by himself. His spirit needs nurturing as well as the wife's. He also has emotions, and having a belligerent wife and family members distressing him, expecting too much from him alone, he will break and may give up totally.

(5) Lack of understanding and appreciation for the husband's gentle, loving, faithful, loyal, and quiet disposition, is often a turn off for abusive women. They do not see these character traits as great strengths to be appreciated and adored.

I have witnessed repeatedly with a broken heart the mistreatments of these kinds of men by their abusive wives. I often wondered how many times the situation is reversed for women of the same gentle dispositions are abused by rough and insensitive men. And here are women who have such men with quiet and loving temperaments, whom they greatly unappreciated, misrepresented, and mistreated.

When I was a very young girl, I had a shocking experience that never left me. There was an old man in our community, Mr. Magot, who always appeared to be very emaciated and very sick most times. We were very good friends. He was always pleasant to me and treated me as his daughter. This man died and I was very sad. One day on my school break I decided to visit his home. I saw his wife, Margaret, who was very sick and dying. I sat outside the house next to her bedroom door. She immediately was glad to see me and opened up—rather confessed to me her cruel and unjust treatment to her husband. I was shocked. She continued to confess as though she was talking to an adult. I did not know what to do with all this information. She confessed her infidelities, how she overworked him, starved him, and did not appreciate his kind and gentle spirit, deprived him of love, and never say to him before his death "I am sorry." She confessed the worst things to me and how she wanted to die and could not die.

I left shocked and shaken and told no one of this experience after that, until the writing of this book. I felt it was too horrible news to speak of. However, it shaped my perception of the kind of woman, lover, and wife I will not be. Even though I was in an abusive relationship, I often remembered this experience, and chose not to retaliate too much when I knew I could (in the worst ways); but rather leave because I know the Father has out there a man for me with the kind, gentle, fidelity, loving, hardworking, and pleasant disposition who will not mistreat me, nor instruct me to hurt others. That kind of man I crave to have in my life and love. So why waste time with Mr. Ruffian, or Mr. Cruel.

Chapter six

SELF-SACRIFICE

The Savior extended himself in love and taught us how to extend love to others. Humans cannot sacrifice themselves to accomplish what He did. He loved the whole world and gave His life for our sins. That giving of life was not self-sacrifice or He would have nothing else to give. We are to choose to love harmoniously, peacefully, freely from distresses, diseases, unfaithfulness, and hostility.

Our communities are to be places of refuge and strength for our families and friends away from the daily stresses of life. And normally the only reason for stress, not distress, are as a result of outside influences—arrogant neighbor, ill health, loss of employment, etc., that seems to want to pervade our lives. Yet, these outside influences by themselves do not make matters worse. We can overcome many difficulties by working together and utilizing correct help and resources available, and not allowing any situation to distract from our healthy goals to be happy.

One of the main reasons things get worse is the desire for one partner to blame the other for causes and ill effects. They chose not to see the remedies within themselves, together, and there exist that evil desire to oppress the other for each difficulty. Where once was seen love and hope in each other both are replaced by something incomprehensible, too deep to fathom and too dark to sort through. As a result of nurturing wrong values in our lives we expose the home to attacks of the enemy. When we ignore correct principles, our character become transformed into something ugly which can be difficult for others to live with.

Many kinds of basely attitudes develop as a result of wrong values associated with marriage an "institution," and as self-sacrifice used as methods of escaping responsibilities from freedom for personal growth.

These are some of the many methods of escaping responsibilities from freedom for personal growth:

A. ***Masochism*** *(moral)*: The person(s) of abuse always feels responsibility for the abusive situations deriving from the abuser. They fear any form of healthy confrontations from anyone who cares to intervene to bring about healthy solutions for everyone's well-being. They delight in the oppressor's ill compatibilities and compare them to their own and determine through religious reasoning that staying with the abusers is proof that they are better than the abusers, and that abuse can be tolerated for marriage to last, as an example. At the expense to their own worth and safety they become dependent on their continuous compulsive sacrificing of their own needs to those of the abusers and others, often at the cost of considerable suffering, shame, and abuse. They will express symptoms of suffering, may seek help knowing their true source of suffering, but will not put forward their real source of pain to get help. They rationalize it would be too much work and pain to sort through, the abuser may be too difficult to work with, and that the environment might become unsafe.
B. ***Sadism*:** This psychological perversion is not only reflected in the abuser for their love of cruelties inflicted on the victims, but also through the behavior of their victims. The victims rationalize the cruelties inflicted on them are expression of true love, which they know are not but do not look for ways to escape. They also adopt a religious mentality in creating distress by inflicting continuous guilt and shame on their partners instead of finding ways to better their own lives.

C. ***Destructiveness***: The victims of abuse who adopt this kind of behavior behave impulsively without thinking of their actions and possible consequences. When displeasure occurs they will look for ways to destroy themselves, their partners, and others around them in thoughts, deeds, and speech. They see themselves as the only victim in their situation and look for others around them to destroy. Others are of no value and their suffering of no consequence to them, even of those who are defenseless and are dependent on them for survival.
D. ***Automaton conformity.*** These are neurotics whose loyalty and affectionate behavior often conceal that powerful desire to submit themselves constantly to their spouse to the point of subjugation extending out to abusive authorities. This kind of submission can be very destructive in a passive way wanting others to depend on them, preventing true growth of others. They do this at the cost of their own authority. There are others who are so passive they lack a strong revolve toward anything and can easily be controlled by others. To them this kind of submission makes it easy to avoid any kind of "negative" response or abusive behavior from the spouse.

Many individuals are afraid of prerelationship and premarital counseling. They see it as trampling on their rights, are afraid of exploring and correcting wrong values, and refuse opportunities for improvements. Although education does play a role, true wisdom in knowing true principles is an imperative in understanding right values. To learn these principles and have them in our soul to transform our character in communicating with each other from the heart, most people are lazy to know how and to try.

Many married individuals who claimed they are abused are actually inflicting abuse on themselves. In part due to wrong values been taught or adopted. The negative attitudes toward their own spouse, who are doing their best only results in the breaking down of communications and affections. Regardless of culture, bad attitudes, and wrong values do exist.

The words values and abuse are not welcome in our society. We all want right values and no one rightly wants abuse. Yet, if right values are explored and communicated deeply before marriage, there should be no reason for abuse. Most people in society sees them as *private affair,* and we are all impacted when it does happen. Some leaders in our society are afraid to talk about them. They all claim that everyone is entitled to their own values because the marriage is an *institution* and it is dangerous idea to interfere, and the abuser can do as they please. They are afraid to teach against it to openly bring awareness of this evil and to correct wrong conducts.

The absence of right values is abuse when not enforced in the communities and in the home, character of individuals will break down.

Right values are based on the Creator's principles—commandments, laws, statutes, and judgments—right foundation to build our growth on. These principles are to counsel us when we are confused, discouraged, depressed, and to help keep us stable in good and bad times. They pull us back when we are going the wrong way, prevent us from doing evil acts, and help us to identify the good in our mates who love us deeply and need space to communicate it.

Many victims of abuse are revictimized by some members of their communities and are pushed back to the abusers and are perceived as potential burden to others. They are not counseled to see their own self-worth, potentials, and abilities for successes, and the abusers were neither reprimanded of their evil acts nor counseled to become good. It is a fearful situation.

These victims of abuse are told they must return because "you made a vow." The statement: "You made a vow," becomes in this case a burden heavier to carry than the abusive situation. It tells victims and witnesses that there really is no hope for any safety in marriage from abuse. The abusers are glorified that they have the power to be the leader in the home and no matter what the wrongs or how perilous the situation, their victims must return home; to be under their control, continuously, because they are under no obligation to behave rightly and the victims are defined by them as "property," not a person.

While speaking with a friend, the abuser kept declaring that "property is nine-tenth of the law and I must stay with him." My friend boldly said, "No, your wife is an adult! She is not a child, nor your child! If you do not stop your cruel behavior she must leave! You are very cruel and she is not responsible for your abusive behavior to her and toward others!" He was most unhappy and quiet. Then my friend asked me, "What do you want to do?" I replied, "I want to leave." He agreed. This friend was most grieved of the continuous abuse inflicted on me and on some of his community members by this abuser.

Many adult victims of abuse tolerate abuses and call this endurance, patience, love all equivalent to "self-sacrifice," believing it is better than not having a partner. In reality they are sacrificing everything good in themselves, their environment, and others most often the children for something that is far less satisfying and destructive. If you choose this, there is no room in an abusive environment for loving yourself or to extend love to others in clean and healthy ways. You are in a stagnant growth, unable to move beyond your limited visual capabilities staying in such misery.

All my life I could never see the benefit to victims of domestic abuse. Their whole being suffers intensely. Worst of all their children suffer and are also re-victimized by society. As a result they appear to not have a fighting chance for good health and success in life unless family members, friends, neighbors, and the community intervene. Also the adult victims need help to see beyond themselves and reach out to their children. They must determine in their mind that all forms of abuse must cease immediately and protect the children at all cost.

We choose to love because it feels good, and we grow because of it. We know the person(s) we are extending love to will grow into that wonderful human being we so want to see in our society to be at peace with themselves, us, and each other. We want our beloved to be free to reach for and connect with Our Creator who only can teach us true love.

Submit, Compromise, and Subjugation

Many individuals use the word "submit" without clear interpretations and illustrations as giving oneself totally to another; giving up their own powers of reasoning to another human being, and allow someone else to be totally in charge. Humanly it is not possible. Every human being needs freedom to extend themselves to others, in healthy and clean relationships; friendships and family, for example. They often equate *submit to compromise and subjugation*. The misinterpretations and the misapplications of these three words used to define intimate relationships often prove to be the catastrophic components in a marriage. Rarely the newlyweds today are taught how to really communicate with each other from the heart.

Webster's Dictionary defines:

"Submit," *v.t. put forward for consideration; surrender own ideas for consideration.*

"Compromise," *meeting halfway, coming to terms by giving up part of a claim.*

Internet definition—http://dictionary.reference.com/browse/Subjugation defines:

"Subjugation," *n., the act, fact, or process of subjugating, or to bring under control; conquer; enslavement, overthrow, beating, oppression or conquest; the act or process of bringing someone or something under one's control; put down by force or intimidation; forced control by others.*

Submit in any relationship mean: the willingness to respectfully, lovingly, and harmoniously reason together combining ideas to be worked out for the benefit of each other. Compromise means the same thing taking it further by meeting each other halfway to make an idea work. What one person cannot do the other may be able to do, or get help to develop the idea, make it workable for the given situation and for the desired effects. If the ideas are proven not good, then they are dismissed, or been reconsidered for another situation, time, and place.

The abuser had the wrong idea of submit and suddenly in a fierce manner demanded to be called "master." Well, I corrected him on that. He tried again another time with the attempt to physically assault me and I stood my ground. I chose to obey our Heavenly Father at all cost to obey his commands: *thou shall have no other Gods before me*, and He was very compassionate when He said it because He knew the hearts of those who want to be worshipped are evil. My worship is to be always voluntarily and lovingly, that is why He is my loving master.

No one has total power or authority to control another in such a negative way. There must be mutual trust, respect, and safety.

No one in their right mind should ever call an abuser "master." That is to surrender all of self and autonomy to the every whim of the abuser who does not love you and want to be thinking and making decisions for you. You are canceling the rightful authority in your life for another.

To call a lover/spouse "master" by your own choice is: to bear witness of the fact that the lover/spouse is a truly loving person and has mastered the art of loving you and does not mistreat others. You must have safety and great joy in your spouse to do this.

Premeditated Murder

This form of sin—abuse—is premeditated murder. Exodus 20:13: "Do not murder."

Pina shared her story of how intensely abusive her husband was to her. So abusive that it was an all-out war he declared on her publicly and privately. She was constantly physically abused in private and more so in public. What made her return to the abuser was the constant revictimization she experienced from a religious leader who reminded her of her "vows." He repeatedly told her, "It is better to have a husband than none at all, men are hard to come by, and no man would want you with children."

Get real. This religious leader did not know his own vows to our Creator and to society to have the good sense to know what a marriage vow is. He used his religious authority to generate fear in the abused. He clearly was insulting her, indicating to her that she was not worth real love, and that no man would love her after having a husband and children. He saw her as unclean and unlovable. This is what some religious teachers teach. Yet most of these kinds of leaders are having adulterous relationships outside their own marriage and they know this too is wrong.

A cruel leader once said, "It is the duty of the wife who is abused to live a life of humility, praying constantly, always respecting the abuser that he will turn around." They also in their own false teachings replace God's authority in the home for the authority of the abuser.

Did our Creator not cry out to all community leaders: *"Hear now, O head of Jacob, and you rulers of the house of Israel: Is it not for you to know justice?"—**Micah 3:1.*** All this still applies today.

Today, are there not existing leaders after His covenant to Jacob? Leaders in all levels of communities and especially religious communities do have greater responsibilities in bringing justice to the oppressed. After discussing abuse with individuals and leaders in society who are not associated with religion; they are most empathetic. They in detail explained the psychological, physical, emotional, and social ill effects of abuse. They can illustrate to you how individuals, families, and all levels of communities are destroyed by this evil call abuse. Yet when discussing the matter with some religious leaders they are most callous and cruel toward victims of abuse, especially toward children who become fatherless as a result of such cruel treatments by abusers and these leaders' rejection of them.

This form of sin—abuse—is premeditated murder. **Exodus 20:13:** "Do not murder."

Why I call it that? To abuse someone is to slowly kill all harmony; joy, peace, love, body, and hope in that individual. It says to the individual "You are not worth anything, you are not valuable, you will never succeed." The abuser wants the victim(s) to give up on everything good in life, to live a life of sheer hell and great darkness. The result is death in self-worth and to your true identity in your Creator, death in potentials to contribute greatly to society, and death to the body slowly. The abuser's intent is to destroy you physically and mentally, to kill you slowly, and you will die eventually. This is the result intended.

For many years I have observed many widows and widowers who abused their spouse are highly honored in society. So honored they should be given a plaque or a monument built in their honor. They know what they did was evil. These individuals hold dear "until death do us part," is simply that, "until death do us part," as a weapon of mass destruction against their spouse. They know they do not love their spouse but will never let them go.

They do this because they rather see them dead than be free to succeed either by themselves, with others, or with another partner. They witness the suffering of their spouse for years and deliberately will do nothing to relieve the suffering. They wait until it is too serious and too late to be cured, then go crying to their community for prayer repeatedly while they constantly and privately are exulting in the suffering of their spouse. At the very end they try to advocate for the physical recovery of the ailing spouse, yet when you tell them the right thing to do to ease their spouse's suffering they nauseatingly refuse to do it, or they will give you the impression that they are trying.

They pretend they are trying but in actual fact they are actively and deliberately causing the suffering to increase daily. They will daily watch their spouse die, and pretend they were there for them all along. In this situation, the spouse is physically there, but they have already divorced the spouse by detaching themselves, and now waiting for death of the spouse to honor their wicked intentions. Of course no one in society will ever know, so they think, that they have deliberately killed their spouse—they know that the suffering was a direct result of the abuse inflicted on them.

They want most of all to be honored as a widow/widower and not as a divorcee. These individuals are repulsed by the very thought of divorce, especially if they were married before. They reasoned within themselves it would not look good to be divorced again, so they prefer to cover up their shame with violence-murder-false honor.

Yet there are foolish single individuals in all communities who will pursue such individuals as potential mates. They believe this person will always be supportive to them in the way they fooled society they were for their ailing spouse. It is nice to have someone to be there for you, but this in itself is a death trap.

A slow death by the hands of the abuser is currently not defined as murder in our current laws. The Creator's principles—commandments, laws, statutes, and judgments defined this behavior as murder; and the criminal law should define it as murder. Even if the victim does not die immediately, it should be defined as attempted murder, because it is the intent of the abuser that their victims die, and most victims of abuse eventually die as a result of trauma inflicted by abusers. It is equivalent to been held captive by an outside enemy and are tortured daily until you die.

Too many people in society continue to live in very distressful situations and not experiencing good health. All medical specialists and frontline workers; cardiologists, psychiatrists, psychologists, internists, counselors, chiropractors, neurologists, social workers, haematologists, naturopathic doctors, police, EMS personnel, counselors, etc., will have testimonies to these facts of victims who had, and are still suffering from chronic exposure to distressful abusive situations. They most times are overwhelmed with such cases and sometimes refer them to other medical and counseling specialists. Daily, more people are dying for lack of right love, rather than material or financial wealth.

Chapter seven

RECOGNIZING YOUR RED SEA

To recognize your Red Sea is to be in a position where you have come to at the edge of the "*road,*" nowhere else to go, you cannot look back, and you are not safe to stay there. You have passed your level of endurance and will break or die if you continue in it. You know it because you are been heaped on emotional, physical, psychological, and spiritual pain for such a long time you feel in your soul and every fiber of your being you will die soon without any hope of experiencing true freedom, true quality of living, opportunities to see your children grow up, and worst of all that hopelessness of never to experience eternal life.

Make no mistake about this: In an abusive home, you and your children are prisoners of war. The devil, its host, and the abuser have waged war against you and will not stop until you are dead. Then another victim is targeted. You are in a fight for you and your children's life and trying to make sense of it is futile. While in this dark place of abuse your lifespan is greatly reduced, and you will not have enough energy to reason your way out of it. The enemies of your soul hate you intensely and you must escape.

This war is not based on facts. Your sweet personality and bad cooking have nothing to do with it. It is simply the nature of the abuser and because you have cried out to the Creator of the universe—our Heavenly Father for help you are been directed to your Red Sea.

This Red Sea may appear to be another existing challenge faced by the oppressed. A problem because they know it is the only way of escape. It appears to expand to the breadth and depth of the earth. It never seems to end, with no shore in sight, and only a glimpse of the horizon with no sunrise or sunset and may look dark. This Red Sea can be black, fast, and furious as Niagara Falls in a stormy night. Or it can be constant and calm but the currents are more powerful than the fastest and strongest swimmer can endure. Should you start to swim hoping a shore will exist soon, or hoping to just float on your back the waves and the undercurrents are too powerful to endure and will wear you out.

Hoping to see shore is hoping for help to arrive soon, or hoping the troubles will not last too long. The waves are the constant reminders of abuses you hope to overcome along the way, and the troubles to face, but might eventually reach the other side. The undercurrents are the reminders of the strength of the oppressor—the force of the blows, the violent words, the weapons of mass destruction in your present situation used to weigh and keep you down. The different faces of oppression—people who you will meet want to tell you to stay in your abusive home and the reminder of the abuser telling you, "You will never make it on your own out there without them." That same blatant lie that is been rehearsed to all victims, as though the abuser is God. So then, at what cost will the abused be scared enough to stay at the shores of their Egypt, or take their chances in their Red Sea and flee. Some friends and family may also say, "Too much legal difficulties, your health will suffer, etc.," they will use to discourage you from trying.

But in your Egypt, cascades of troubles have been heaped on you greatly taking its toll, and great distresses are more intensified preventing you from recognizing yourself as once the person who dreamt of freedom to dance, to be loved, and to love. The children too are experiencing extreme pain, and may see their Egypt as a mountain too high to climb, too wide to walk around, too steep to trek, and too cloudy to see each mountain table top. The rock is the abuser on dry land—Egypt, where there is no peace. The abused appear to be caught between a rock and deep sea and cannot return there or will continue to suffer more severely and that is sure death. You fear to step in your Red Sea because you are not sure of your skills and resources to make it across.

Remember the oppressed multitude of slaves how they too feared their Red Sea? It was no little thing for them. This was serious and intense to the maximum, a real crisis. It was as surreal as any moment of escaping for one's life can get. Their Red Sea was a literal sea they could touch and hear the waves, but it was not a place for them to swim in. They would not make it across as they were too weak, worn out, and oppressed to even try. They became extremely fearful and instantly rationalized that it was better for them to remain on dry and familiar ground back to the abuser and the abusive environment, instead of facing this obstacle. It was a mammoth of a problem never faced in all their past generations, and they despaired and accused Moses of bringing them there to die out there in the Red Sea. This Red Sea appeared too furious and frightening to them, and they were too tired and burnt out to even bother with it.

They were too weak to cry out for help and Moses interceded on their behalf for deliverance, and because our Creator understood their distresses their Red Sea was parted for them. They literally, physically stood and watched the Red Sea parted and the safety provided for them while crossing through on dry land, and realized it was not as scary as they thought as the fears they imagined began to disappear were quickly replaced with feelings of exhilaration too powerful to describe.

The purpose of your Red Sea is the Creator's battlefield where He fights for you.

He could and can victoriously fight for you while in your Egypt. However, Egypt—abusive environment is not where He wants you, nor where He wishes to continually exert his energy to make you strong to endure abuse continuously. It is not a place where He will play referee between you and the abuser hoping he/she will come good—and will not.

He allowed this Red Sea to exist to show you a better option of survival. There He will meet the enemy on His term. It is not intended for the abuser to join you to continue hurt on you, but a way out only for *your* deliverance/escape. If the enemy comes after you then it becomes His battlefield against them where He will destroy them.

Chapter eight

FACE YOUR RED SEA

To face your Red Sea is good. It is a place to be as scary as it may look and feel. The Red Sea is only the difference between you staying and dying, move on and live. It represents the possibility of what lies beyond the horizon—peace, normal daily struggles of life, and starting all over, etc. If you look good at where the horizon should be, that is where the sun rises and sets—over there, not where you are. Victims of abuse looked for that ray of hope for a long time, to bloom in its sunshine, but they were caused to not see or trust it. Beyond the horizon awaits your dreams to be attempted and be fulfilled. Do not plan to die in your shattered shelter of broken dreams, where there exists no peace and joy, with no normal everyday struggles of life.

Plan to live and die where the sun rises and sets,
where peace and joy dwells and when the rain
stops falling you can see your way clearly.

Invite your children to join you in that desire to dream what seems the impossible dream. The inability to do this is to live a life of distress, horror, and constant grief needlessly. Give your children hope and they will learn they can prosper and were not created to live in distress. A wonderful Creator created them to be happy in whatever town, city, or country they live in, and when He sees them suffering He wants to take them out and lift them beyond danger where they cannot be reached nor be separated from Him. To not be reached is to be in a position in life where you are free to develop a close relationship with the Creator to learn of Him and of yourself. As a result you will be more mature, educated, at peace with yourself and others, and be able to make important choices for your life.

At this time you may think you are not mature or sane enough to deal with such distressful situation. No one is mature, skilled, sane, or educated enough to stay and succeed in this darkness. It is totally against human nature, or you would not suffer the way you are. Theorists and theologians can talk all they want but they do not have the power to balance emotions with abuse.

When you are experiencing abuse, your integrity is broken down daily. No amount of facial makeup or expensive clothing can hide it. No level of education can help you hide the deep pain you feel inside. Some people might not be able to tell by looking at you. However, as the time of abuse prolongs so does your pain. I often heard this phrase *"Your eyes are a mirror to your soul."* That is a fact. No amount of eye makeup can deflect or suppress the sadness that wants to emanate from your soul to the outside world. You will also act it out in ways you cannot always predict and avoid. Feelings of pain can cascade in episodes of distressful behavior which are automatically interpreted as call for help.

When someone is truly happy it shows. It reflects a natural beauty from within and an outward expression of peace overflowing outward that cannot be explained. Even when out of sorts in normal situations this peaceful disposition will naturally flow from within you. People will recognize it and be happy for it.

In your abusive situation you lack the opportunity and freedom to be the mature, graceful, natural and beautiful person He designed you to be. His plans for you are peace, joy, and success, not for your destruction totally opposite to what He desires for everyone.

You know it because you feel it in your soul. You question yourself every day—"Why is my life like this, I need to succeed why can I not, when will I be happy again?" When you leave this abusive situation you will have the chance to grow in His character. You will know the difference between true and fake love; and be able to discern more easily these character traits in people you will meet, will not fear to question them and if necessary avoid them. This experience will help you to determine in your mind not to ever return to anything that look, walk, sound, talk, smell, feel like, or anything else you came out of or witnessed others go through. You will be more educated and free to learn of correct principles will help build those boundaries that were not in place which resulted in your subjugation to this dark life of abuse.

Your maturity and education can be reality as you purpose in your mind to learn from your mistakes and grow into the person you were created to be in His design for you. It will show. Your children will see it in you and want to attain it. This maturity and education will begin from doing the right things to get out and to stay free from any potential future abusers.

Everyday remind your children of people who love them—their Creator, friends, families, and connect them to look forward to belonging again this time without interruptions. Remind them of what it is to laugh, dance, love, and be loved by others and they can desire safety in freedom to learn of their great individual potentials and abilities to succeed. Be accountable to them so they can trust and respect you.

ACCEPT YOUR RED SEA

This is your Red Sea, unique to you and your children in your specific situation. Your Egypt was designed against you to break and eventually kill you but your Red Sea is here to get your attention to give you a choice for hope and a better future, and your children need your help to understand and accept it to be hopeful. You can choose to cry for yourself only or be angry enough to want you and your children out at all cost.

Your Red Sea represents the end of your abuse. You are at the edge of this dark and mere existence with nothing to offer you exist here and you realize you cannot go back and must continue forward.

When you accept this Red Sea, you will begin to feel in your soul a separation from your Egypt, and new anxieties will exist in the anticipation of getting out. The fear of leaving may seem to override the fear of staying. These new anxieties are many emotions combined—fear, joy, anger, resentment, hatred are to be recognized, embraced, and sorted out. They may come in waves as you will feel them knowing you are fed up with where you are.

To watch the dignities of your children stripped away each day is heart rendering, as each day's records ends in abuse. They are fearful of everything and everyone, and may withdraw from you *and appear* impossible to deal with. They are simply trying to deal with this fierce situation all by themselves because they may perceive that they are becoming a burden to you. But you must continue to get help for their sakes. They are counting on that and need your continued encouragement and attention. You need to extend yourself to them in love and empathy realizing they are suffering with you and have more difficulties understanding why it happened. They may internalize the situation and emotions blaming themselves and withdrawing attempting to find their own solutions to these problems on their own. Do not allow them to withdraw, nor to blame themselves and internalize these problems.

While experiencing such trauma your Red Sea may appear darker, uninviting, and dangerous, possibly more dangerous than what you are presently in because the situation has prolonged beyond what you can endure and the abuser is becoming increasingly insecure.

It is a place which requires an immediate decision to physically step out into the unknown toward the possibilities.

The decision to leave does not come without challenges but lives are at stake.

You may realize, "yes," there are painful steps to make, but must be made. It is a real world where possibilities do exist, and leaving your Egypt—abusive home not an option.

You are desperate to move forward without the possibilities while expecting the impossibilities.

You know what you want and realize there are potential obstacles and failures along the way: health issues, legal battles, finances, time, etc. However, you decide it is better to fail trying than not at all. Failures can occur in trying, but it is the attempt which can be very rewarding, and the eventual successes, even in failures because you will learn new skills which will lead to the best quality of life you desperately need for you and your children, and is attainable.

Chapter nine

TIME TO TAKE A STAND

After recollecting yourself you realize who you were, what you have become, and who you can be. You decided to make a decision. Steps must be made. After following all good advice and putting it all together in ways workable, now you realize you have a new focus. No longer will you need to constantly defend yourself against the abuser.

You have something—a gold mine—diamonds.

Diamonds: your true potentials, freedom, children's future to fight for and you leave immediately or set yourself a deadline to step in that Red Sea.

You realize it is one thing to be poor, and it is another to be embarrassed because of it and that you and your children can be content because you already have the skills to make it happen, and you will be free to learn new ones without duress and fear.

You are now realizing that you and your children were not alone all this time, your Red Sea is a better place, there are some good people out there, and that regardless of their faults some people in the world do care. It is at this point you may have a place to go or not, but knowing where to go is detrimental: a safe place, a friend, family member, another apartment or a shelter.

You may not at this time have the courage to take that stand but others who witness your disparities are hurting for you and will take that stand for you.

I always thought we were alone until while witnessing what was the abuser's last grandstanding to degrade us, my friend Diana, boldly went up to his face, toe-to-toe with him, very boldly and in a loud voice, shouted, "Comgin, do what you know you have to do!" Immediately the darkness that clouded my decision to leave was lifted.

When someone shows they care it is as the correct fuel to your car's engine. You are now powered and energized to take that stand, walk, or run for your life. I was encouraged to take that giant leap of faith, knowing anything is better than this.

The abuser tried several times to get me fired. He repeatedly would stalk me at work and one time he without provocation verbally assaulted the staff and immediately I was fired. The day after losing, I attended a group discussion with some friends discussing forgiveness; they asked me why I looked so sad. I simply replied, "I believe in forgiveness and all that but the way I feel now I am in the mood to go to prison and will not regret it. Do not talk to me about forgiveness right now because what someone did to me yesterday I am beside myself with what I feel!" They were horrified and asked me to explain what happened.

They were very supportive of me, and while explaining the situation to them the abuser began walking over to find out what I could possibly be saying, a gentleman stood up and signaled to him not to. He stayed back. For weeks after they were a very strong support for me.

They encouraged me to leave, "Hurry and get out of this kind of life. Get out and allow no one to bring you and your child down. You do not need a house, even a small place is better than this." They extended their help even further and others joined them in giving us support. Had it not been for the support of these men, I would have an insatiable hatred toward men after leaving the abusive home.

They continued to pray about my situation and two days after the staff at work called me. Without discussing my situation to them they explained the situation and their acknowledgement of his abusive tendency toward me why he was stalking me. They rehired me immediately. The entire staff at the company took a very strong stand for me against the abuser allowing me the freedom to be safe. They made sure he was not allowed on the property nor in the building, and made sure after work I would leave on time to attend my other part time work, and they also made sure he was not following me.

My late friend, Mr. Greene, a few months before he died, heard of this situation and approached the abuser—"I heard you are abusing your wife. I want to talk to you." Before he could finish his sentence the abuser quickly ran away, and always careful to avoid him afterward.

People can grieve so intensely on your behalf that it does spill out publicly. Allow them the space and freedom to do so on your behalf. A group of people had witnessed our disparities one day while observing his rude behavior towards us they were so full of anger and grief that they approached him and shouted loudly, for all to hear. "Shut up, stop mistreating your family. We are tired of your behavior toward your family!" They had witnessed his abusive behavior toward us and their soul could not contain it anymore and exploded in anger and intense grief.

People looked expecting me to defend and protect, but I refused.

If you are still unsure how to take your stand that is not unusual. Do not be afraid. This is a war like no other. You are not fighting against a physical enemy that is controlling your spouse. This enemy is a frightful and powerful foe that will do anything to distract you at all cost.

Take a stand in your faith, knowing that there is a Higher Power—the Heavenly Father, our Creator of all who can fight for you and keep you stable.

A stranger named Corine had experienced this situation and became extremely discouraged. I encouraged her to take a stand in what she knows about her Creator and how He had helped others. I reminded her of His love and is not happy to see His creation been abused in anyway. She was encouraged by this and realized how precious she is, and not to be treated in any cruel manner. She took her stand, left, and as a result of intensive counseling, the husband repented and they reconciled.

He will do anything to protect you, even if He must take you out of the abusive home. He is not limited to His own laws. He wants you to wake up to the realization that you are precious, made in His own image. No one has the authority or power to be cruel to you in anyway. To be abused means that the enemy wants to replace the Creator's rightful place in your life and cause you to give up on life, and to destroy you completely. The abuser is out of order; their entire being is not operating in rightful sequence and harmony as designed by the Creator.

Deliberately turn your attention to the Creator who only can keep you calm, safe, and focused. Realize that the battle is not ours. Only He can see the enemy, and empower you to take a stand against it. Take some time and worship Him. **Second Chronicles 20:16-17**—"The battle is not yours, it is the Lord's." Worship Him, praise Him. Believe and have faith in your Heavenly Father and He will teach you how to be successful His way. Give thanks to Him and He will frighten the enemy for you. He alone has total power, authority, and victory.

Tell Him exactly what you want to say and really want. You are in a sticky situation where you cannot say out loud what your plans are.

In order to participate in the victory He plans for you, ask Him for help in what you say to the abuser and anyone else, how and when you say it. You are tempted to announce you want to be out of there whenever, but you know you are not safe to express it.

Abusers do not care about their victims wanting to decide to leave and end this relationship with them. They are not thrilled in losing their long-held power over their victims.

They will not like the fact and the message that you no longer will tolerate having being manipulated, that is not your problem, but they must get the message. Plan to leave and limit or completely cut off (if possible) your interactions with the abusers. They are a danger to themselves and to society.

Chapter ten

RECOGNIZING YOUR POWER OF ANGER

When you begin to talk with people about your situation, you not only realize you must do something to get out but that you are learning to use that anger positively to propel you to move away from it.

This kind of anger is not of revenge to hurt the abuser nor to target anyone to replace the object of your anger. This anger is the result of analyzing your situation; causes, affects, and outcomes. What is worst; leave, or stay and die in this abusive situation. It is the result of your self-evaluation, children's state of mind, and of your immediate life. Realizing and accepting against all odds your true value as a human being, your great potential to your own family and society that will propel you to want this stumbling block out of your way at all cost.

The cost in this case is the loss of a companion through separation/ divorce, loss of a home, finance, material things, etc. But when you truly think things through, all these things are replaceable at a better time in your life. You now realize you are dying staying in the abusive environment as you become more aware of your increase zealousness for life and begin to ask yourself many questions as you become aware of opportunities lost for growth.

You have dreams and visions of success whether it is a project, a career, or whatever you know will help mankind and you are rebuffed by an abusive spouse, it is not good. Words of discouragement will only lead to intense frustration and anger.

When you get to this point of realizing your power of anger inside of you, it will propel you to no longer listen to lies of the abuser. They have no power and choose to abuse you in diminishing your self-confidence to make them seem powerful. Without you appearing to be powerless the abuser cannot feel powerful. Everything and everyone must move and be according to their dictates, assumptions, and accusations, very destructive to everyone and everything in their environment.

Abusers may impose religious creeds to express their own fears to manipulate their victims' obedience without freedom to express love creatively is cruelty in the attempt to replace the Creator's true authority in themselves and their environment. They want you to remove yourself from His presence and directions, love, joy, and peace, and to be controlled by them.

Analyze lies abuser speaks/shouts at you, there is great fear behind all of that. Lies especially through abuse is designed to break the will of the victims which can propel you to do what is necessary to leave. Your actions or inactions in this case are very powerful. The abuser knows you are smart and if given a chance to succeed, the sky and all the galaxies beyond will be the limits for you.

Words are very powerful. Words brought beautiful worlds and universes into existence and creating you the unique individual. "Let there be light, plants, animals, etc." No hands on necessary. Words cause and break wars, healing and destruction, divide and unite friends and families, bring about many wonderful activities in this world to make it a better place.

Words of the divine Creator created you, and you can say with King David, ***"I am fearfully and wonderfully made."*** You are special. Your Creator is king of all worlds and universes and you are His children.

We are royalty and must live good quality lives to the best of our abilities. Who dare messes with His creation?

The words "you will never make it on your own, you will not live a day out there without me" are nothing but lies. These very words abusers use in the attempt to keep victims imprisoned. You start to realize if living in this hell is living, it is dying at its worst. You cannot always choose how you will die, but you can choose how to live.

You are desperate for a life free from unnecessary distress, a place for restoration, peace, and live without a cantankerous spouse and fear of the children been abused. This peace is healing of the mind for you and your children, absence of abuse, the ability to see your way clearly, make your own mistakes, laugh, and learn, and the ability to cope with the everyday normal stresses of life, experience complete healing, and teach your children how to live good quality lives.

This good quality of life is where they are connected to the Creator to learn from Him, begin the journey of healing and success, experience peace of mind, and learn to dance. You must explain to them that the separation from the abuser and the abusive environment will be painful but they will heal. As they become accustomed to a new home free of the abuser and abuse their brain and nerves will calm down and healing will take place in a timely process. It is not a fantasy. It is reality. We do not need statistics to tell us the success rate of us and our children leaving an abusive home. These statistics have no place with you because they will not be allowed to mold you and your family's future and character. The statistics are too often misused by society and other authorities to quash your future and cause you to see no way out.

There is less success for a child's life in an abusive home than a home without abuse. When such statistics are used inappropriately, it gives more power to the abusers to believe they are of great value to society, no one can live without them, and they need not stop their abusive behavior.

When children live in abusive home their brain is malnourished as there is a famine of love, and lack of appropriate affection which aids proper absorption of nutrients. Fear is what they breathe and exhale, all day and all night. If they are forced to grow up in it too long and not get help, when they are older sometimes unwittingly they are attracted to other abusers and the results are most times tragic.

When you allow yourself to become consciously aware of the deep suffering of the children, allow your soul, body, and mind to cry out and be very angry. This deep hurt you feel is only a fraction of what your children are enduring of which they cannot put in words to express to you or anyone else. The pains they are enduring are suppressed greatly for long periods of times. And as they grow into puberty stages these feelings of pain and anger become more intense, more difficult to identify and express which arrests their normal developmental stages and in some instances can physically cripple or kill them.

If you decide to be angry at the children for their suffering and need for relieve of this burden, you are giving them another burden heavier and more painful to carry than the abuse itself. This will wire their brain wrong and destroying your children.

It is for their benefits that while in the abusive home you allow them the freedom to frequently talk of their painful experiences and to express their emotions, and after leaving, immediately help them more to continue to be relieved of this heavy burden to begin healing and restoration.

Do not allow yourself the false luxury of weighing the evidences to be a referee between the children and the abuser. Do not do it. If the children see you are trying to determine their possible behavior that may have caused criminal behavior from the abuser they will perceive you do not care and will feel revictimized by you. Can you afford to have them hurt because of your ignorance when help is available?

Deliberately choose to put their safety above the fears and possible violent reactions from the abuser and seek help. When you help the children to express themselves they will see through your caring ability and become more aware and angry of the overwhelming injustices and crimes done to them by the abuser and want to leave. Your willingness and ability to get help quickly will help relieve most of the heavy anxieties they carry. They need to experience this from you.

Abusers are not trusted by anyone. I truly believe that when a person chose to abuse, the Creator's blessings for them are put on hold or canceled. He cannot fulfill His promise for them as He really wanted to, because they simply cannot be trusted. They have caused so much pain to His creations that the repercussions seem endless. The pain is deep and often takes a lifetime to heal. Sometimes they are irreparable and cannot be healed in this lifetime.

The Heavenly Father finds no pleasure in abusers as we see in ***Malachi 2:8–9***, He will definitely cut them off from the land of the living. Although He was speaking to abusive nations, He narrows it to all families and individuals. 8.*"If you will not hear, and if you will not take it to heart, to give glory to my name, says the Lord of hosts, I will send a curse upon you, and I will curse your blessings. Yes, I cursed them already, because you do not take it to heart."* 9: *"Therefore I the Lord have made you contemptible and base before all the people. Because you have not kept my ways, but have shown partiality in the law."*

To give glory to His name is to correctly and appropriately represent His character: truth, right love, justice, and safety to His creation. It is also to repent of our wrong ways and maintain that connection with Him through love and obedience to His principles to live right. Showing partiality in His laws means the abuser knows what is right but because of hate for whatever reason the victim(s) bear suffer.

This is reality. When we left, there was first always the fear of this happening again. Our bodies were continuously reacting to every cruel words and actions of abuse. When I dropped a plate or put a cup in a bad spot, I would immediately hear his voice and words of insults poured out on me, and would instantly react to defend myself. This proved that the nervous system was till reacting to chronic exposure to the verbal and physical abuses. I had to remind myself I am no longer there, prayed constantly for God to be in control of my spirit and allow me to hear only His voice and not the voice of the abuser.

For quite a while we continued to suffer emotionally and physically. We both got our own counselor to help us to cope. It does not stop the day you walk out the abusive home. I had to be sensitive to my son and empathize with him each time he reacts. He was very insecure and fearful and doubted I could take care of him by keeping my word to not return to the abuser, and stay free to help him heal completely. Thank God for His healing balm, today, we are no longer in that reactive mode and have successfully healed.

Society has their opinion of success rates after leaving an abuser. You may choose to believe all the statistics but only you can prove it incorrect when you refuse to live by it, and dare do what you dream and obey His instructions. You may be lacking in certain skills but let's face it, they were not taught in the abusive home, neither were they encouraged, why you feel you are lacking them. You lacked the opportunity to tap into your natural gifts to learn and develop them.

Had you pursued your goals the abuser would feel intimidated by your visions. However, had your spouse encouraged you to develop those skills, sharing them with your family would be of benefitted to your spouse.

Do not underestimate the power of Creator's love. His love is pure, true and powerful. You are in this mess not by His choice, but partly by your choice. He will work with you to get out. Your cry for help is His way of stimulating your soul to communicate and give Him permission to work on your behalf. He will send help you never knew existed, and cause the hearts of family members and friends to turn toward you.

Use your anger to propel you to talk to family members you know you can trust. You will be surprised. Do not shut them out, even if they were not close to you before. Let your children know that someone cares about them, they can live healthy lives., The process will be painful for them at first for a little while to be severed from this awful situation but they will heal. They will be healthy again and begin their journey of success. Tell them of your plans to succeed so they will remind you and hold you to it. You must use your anger as motivation to follow through for their survival. If you leave with the desire to succeed you will, regardless of the obstacles

It is awful enough when spouses abuse each other. They can overcome with much counseling and move on positively with their own lives, than the children left to grieve on their own. When the abuser abuses a child who trust them for life itself how much more painful for that child to grieve the abuse or abandonment.

Anger management has its place, but in most part not here. Providing you are not targeting your children with your anger.

Spouses who are separated from their abusive spouse must be vigilant in their anger mismanagement and displacement. They sometimes and quite often see one child as the object of their hate in place of the absent abuser, and show much gentleness to the other. Serious counseling is urgently needed to spare you from sinning against our Creator, oneself, your children, and society.

Abuse and abandonment is not a private affair. It hurt people in and outside your inner circle. Anger mismanagement and displacement are dangerous. It pushes away people who want to be close to you, be your friend, and support you. It causes them to feel ashamed for the support they have given you secretly or openly. They will regret and doubt the prayers they have sent up to the Father in your behalf day and night when they groaned in their spirit interceding for you. It causes you to feel that you are right in whatever abusive statements you make to whoever says whatever that does not stroke the ego and justifies it with anger. "I am the one hurting here." This rage causes you to feel that the whole world is centered on your own circumstances and hurt, with no regard to others who are hurting.

You need your anger not rage to push you. Overwhelming feelings of anger is not unusual. If this rage and all the violent thoughts are nurtured it may cause you to do things that will put your children's future healing in jeopardy. Although you may feel it will help bring about justice, but in the end our children experience no justice in losing you.

The type of anger I am focusing on is *righteous indignation* as a result of the accumulation of years of frustrations, embarrassment, humiliation, hunger, cold, nakedness, and the heaped on of psychological, emotional, financial, spiritual and physical pain to you and your children. Yes, you are extremely angry and rightly so, and you are full and overflowing with all this rubbish and will tolerate no more. This anger will help you to have a strong resolve to put a stop to this immediately. Use your anger to get all help necessary to leave, and it will propel you to leave regardless of the consequences. You choose to refuse to take responsibility for the abuser's misconduct. You refuse to allow your children to be hurt continuously. It must stop! All this bleeding must stop! Immediately!

It is not unusual to want revenge, but you know that is not what will set you free. It will only bring about brief-relief-for-the-moment. After that you are then faced with the awful realization that your children needed you most, and who will see them go through life. Will they heal because the parent they depend on for their security is in prison and the abuser is still free to hurt them? It is best to get the right help and simply walk. By walking away you are teaching them how to allow the Father and the rightful processing of the judicial system to do what is best for them and work out the rest, especially in such painful situations. You are not teaching them to be cowards, but that life must go on for them in a better way, and to immediately begin and continue the journey of healing and restoration.

Chapter eleven

SHADOW

Psalm ***91:1***—*He that dwelleth in the secret place of the Most High shall abide under the shadow of the Almighty.*

To live in the shadow of the Almighty, the Heavenly Father, cannot be compared with the shadow of human beings. It is to put complete trust in Him regardless of how you feel and what your mistakes and circumstances are.

His shadow is protective. With Him you have total safety. The children of Israel lived in His shadow throughout their journey in the wilderness en route to their homeland. His shadow provided shade and protection from the sun's heat and a protective consuming fire preventing the enemy from destroying them and provide warmth during the desert night's cold temperatures.

He is someone who has all power, humility, compassion, and pure love. He cares for you, will never abandon you, and will shield you from every snares of the enemy and when you are experiencing distresses He will guard, heal and preserve your body, mind, and soul and bring people in your life to encourage you. He is accessible twenty-four hours a day, seven days a week. He will hear, answer, and deliver you, will not demean or hurt you in anyway.

In His presence you will never lose your sense of wonder. You are free to give life a fighting chance, dance, love, explore His creation through study, travel, and need own space and opportunities to develop your own skills to your highest potentials.

He made us in His image to reason with Him and grow to be like Him in character because it leads to real growth, and happiness. He is not an idol/image that cannot sympathize with our sufferings. He is a real person and wants us to connect with Him through His principles where we learn:

- His teachings for our own *maintenance and survival*
- *our true identity* in Him
- our *true purpose* in life as He intricately designed us
- to have correct *conceptualization* of who we really are and His concepts of us
- learn our own *self-worth* through His light radiating through us
- *preservation*—how to be preserved until we see His face
- *productivity*—our meaning when we are attached to Him we learn to be of benefit to mankind
- *we learn how to protect life*—how to appreciate every life and not take life or cause anyone to be endangered, and be healthy in every way

In His shadow you are rejuvenated when you wake in the mornings and surprised by His love, grace, and beauty bestowed upon you. You can look in the mirror and say, "I am fearfully and wonderfully made. Who is like you O Lord among all the Lords, there is none like you. You are faithful to put me to sleep and faithful to wake me each next day." You see signs of His love for you and mankind all around you; the flowers, nature, the animals that love to greet you, the birds singing, a homeless person who smiles at you, your children who loves to hug you. You will love and appreciate them daily.

In His shadow people might hate you but you will not care because He will keep you in perfect peace.

When you do wrong you need not run and hide. He wants you to talk it out with Him. Pour your soul out and reconcile back to Him, continue to keep close to Him to experience His rays of love and will reflect outwards to others. It is pure, warm, stimulating to everyone and everything you touch.

Shadow of the Abuser

We live in another shadow as we begin to lose our identity to another. It is to switch our own autonomy and total authority of our lives to another who does not have control of themselves.

Our children living in our shadow is a positive protective love. But to physically keep them with us all their life through compulsion is to subject them to a life of wasting away and death. As they grow we are to release our own limited protective care to the trust of the Almighty, and to gradually release them to other rightful leaders in society to correctly educate them. They learn from us how to trust the Heavenly Father, and learn skills critical to their survival in caring for themselves and mankind. They expand on that knowledge while living outside our protective care, yet needing it occasionally.

In a marriage, or an intimate relationship, it is impossible to be a constant and inseparable companion to another human 24/7. In demanding your where about twenty-four hours a day is preventing you from growing beyond their limited visibilities subjecting you to live under their shadow. They will insist your mannerism be constantly changed to match their own, and any variation is viewed as hostility toward them. They do not appreciate your individual uniqueness and beauty to help contribute to the environment. They want to replace God's beautiful creation, *you*, His masterpiece into something unpleasant, and ugly. This prevents you from developing safe and clean relationships with others. They know they cannot be everything or anything good to you, yet they would not allow you and themselves to grow. They reason, if they cannot grow you must not grow.

It is best when they accept you as you are, encourage and nurture you to grow to your own full potentials. This human shadow is extremely limited and dark in comparison to the shadow of the Almighty.

The children of Israel lived and functioned under the shadow of their oppressor—Pharaoh. That shadow was extremely dark and harmful. So oppressive they could not see beyond their current circumstances and lost all hope of recovery and survival. For many centuries they lost their identity as each generation borne in shackles and chains could only identify with what they saw and experienced.

Pharaoh made sure they were watched 24/7, they had no freedom for worship, healing, growth, education, family healing, prosperity, and rest. The Father was hurt by Pharaoh preventing them from connecting with Him and eventually released them into the wide open where they can connect together and be healed.

In an intimate relationship between man and woman this shadow is also very harmful, unacceptable, and only fosters fearful living with the abuser who is unpredictable and changes like a chameleon. Attempting to live your life for someone else's approval as the defining opinion about yourself you are actually worshipping that person—a form of idol worshipping.

Abusers were never given authority to abuse you and were instead to be the moral leaders in homes and communities, light bearers living in the Creator's presence receiving and giving instructions to others in wisdom, love, prosperity, and peacefulness, etc. The Creator's principles can never be used as tools of offense but for instructions to be internalized for true growth.

Abusers have already removed themselves from the shadow of the Almighty to another source of shadow which only leads to your injuries, subjugating you to live in their fears, of evil ideas, false perceptions, false accusations, and evil influences that were allowed to grow in the abuser. Abusers are on a self-destruct course that the enemy is leading them to take, and no amount of submission can ever pacify them.

This shadow causes you to doubt your own abilities to live a healthy life, limits your freedom for creativity to explore your own abilities to contribute to your communities in large. It can snuff the light of the Heavenly Father from within you, and lead you to a life of degeneration and death.

We feel this type of shadow of the abuser because of the false power they caused us to feel they have over us. This type of shadow can follow you after you leave the abuser because the hurt lingers. And the abusers may insist they keep control over you.

These controls may extend through many forms of abuse through the abuser or their sympathizers. The abusers may want to continue financial control over you causing their shadow to follow you in the form of your financial dependency on them—until you decide to shake them off through your acts of financial independence. They may want to continue to control you through forms of physical, sexual, emotional, psychological, and spiritual abuse by insisting they have access to you and your children to continue their destructive behavior in destroying you. You must get all the help you need to sever those connections at all cost immediately before and after leaving.

After leaving, the abuser tried to insist through the courts and the dormitory school to have physical access to my son but was denied. He wanted to continue hurting my son, but he was protected. He also tried to have access to our residence by using leaders and people in his communities but they were blocked from us. When they tried to communicate with us pretending they were concerned for our safety, I knew they were lying and only wanted access because they never spoke with us before and those who did never liked us.

Many tried to make us feel bad for not communicating with the abuser, wanting me to feel responsible for his well-being, but I did not care to indulge them and defended me and my son against them. They do not care how we were hurting they only wanted us to never forget the abuser as though he is king of the universe.

They may extend their shadows onto you through your children by insisting they keep connected thereby extending their access to you and the children. Help your children to understand this is not healthy for them and they will understand. They may feel fearful and somehow accountable to the abuser because they are young and dependable but you must help them to shake off this negative dependency in their lives by showing them a better way of survival.

Others in our past communities tried to approach my son asking him about his father and wanting him to feel guilty for leaving. Immediately my son would walk them over to me, explain the situation to me, and I put the inquirer in their place. A most unpleasant experience for the inquirers because I had already counseled my son to do this to shake off such continuous oppression following him designed to continue the hurt in him. Once some of such evil inquirers surrounded him to interrogate him and some of his friends immediately came to his aid, and also to tell me what was happening. This incident was quashed right there, immediately.

The constant remembering and reflections of the abusive home and the abuser will also be triggers of stress and a source of shadow over their lives, and they may feel the abuse will continue with you. Items taken from the abusive home may be sources of triggers of PTSD in them. Remove, eliminate, or hide any items that are constant reminders of the abuser and any trauma associated with them. Replace them with fresh, new, clean and better items that bring joy, hope, and love in their lives.

There is no benefit in enduring abuse. Long-term exposure to abuse nullifies the brain and causes chronic pain and as a result we suffer diseases of the body, mind, and soul. Some of the many shadows of abuse lingers in the form of long-term effects of past abuse; PTSD (posttraumatic stress disorder), cognitive distortions, emotional distress, impaired sense of self, avoidance, interpersonal problems.

Psychologists and medical specialists are proving that long-term exposure to distressful situations causes the DNA of our brain responsible for coping with stress can be traumatically altered when exposed to long-term distressful situations, as in abuse. They are successfully linking long-term exposure to distress to bipolar, Alzheimer's diseases, schizophrenic disorders, and many more diseases. They only confirm what we already know because we feel it in our body as a result of been exposed to abuse for long periods of time. Short term exposure to any abuse nullifies the brain.

www.psychologytoday.com/chronicstresscandamagebrainstructureandconnectivity

Constantly pray with them and teach them the loving words of the Savior, our Creator to heal their souls. Expose them to families who are caring to them, help them make better friends, and other activities that will help build their self-worth and promote healing.

Reconnect them to their Heavenly Father in faith organizations that have programs that will help them to heal and divert their attention from the abuser to their Heavenly Father. Abuse was designed to separate them from Him, now they must reconnect to be healed and learn of His true character and their true identity in Him they never knew through abuse.

When abusers behave in controlling, abusive, and possessive manner, they have lost their rightful place. They are alone in their own world of ill perceptions of you, believing the lies they censured against you. This kind of character is destructive. Teach your children that such displaced behavior from the abuser was not appropriate or acceptable and they should stand up against it. This will help them to preserve and maintain their own unique self-separate from the abuser's influence and to discontinue the hurt after leaving, and such behavior will not grow in them nor continue with their future generations.

Counseling immediately after leaving the abusive home and the abuser is imperative for your and their survival. They will need immediate help to heal quickly through correct processes of what was happening to them, how to be more independent in thought, set goals and values, and how to follow through. The pain of abuse will continue to decrease with correct counseling and constant monitoring of their health and your reassurance of your love and support.

We need to talk constantly with the Heavenly Father our Creator for knowledge, understanding, wisdom, and discernment that can only come from a true connection with His principles. Apply them to your lives to help you and your children heal, live harmoniously together, and to help solve your problems one day at a time.

Chapter twelve

VALLEY OF THE SHADOW OF DEATH

This valley of shadow of death you are now experiencing is not easily perceived by others who have not experienced it. Some view this place as a short moment of their life been threatened by an assailant, or when faced with the tragic reality of terminal illness. They are correct.

However, your abusive environment is exactly this—a valley where death does exist because each day you and your children are experiencing distress. This valley is dark and cold, the sun does not shine through to see your way out, and you are certain with your entire being you will die.

Remember the multitude of slaves they too experienced their valley of shadow of death during severe enslavement. They felt there was no way out. The darkness of their valley intensified when Pharaoh out of fear of losing them—his only valuable possessions, intensified his abuse on them to make their escape impossible. He increased their labor by greatly reducing the resources needed to do their jobs effectively, denied them time for worship and for well needed rest, and as their suffering increased he felt more powerful in his ability to facilitate such great pain and suffering.

While you the victim living in this dark valley desperate to leave a series of incidents must happen, whether by self-will of the abuser or supernaturally. When you are constantly with the abuser day in and night out and the abuse keeps increasing you know there is no safe way out. Often the darkness comes before the day—when you are close to your time of freedom the cruelties increases. The abuser may intensify the abuse in various ways he or she may perceive gave them power over you and is in a rush to destroy you as though you are apparently in the most malleable state.

Few months before our escape, the abuser's attitude and cruel actions intensified exponentially on a twenty-four-hour vigil against us. The emotional pain became so intense I was constantly suffering with intense migraines; because my body could not endure the intensity of the emotional abuse as a result it became physical abuse.

I constantly feared for my child's safety when he is alone with the abuser. After obtaining work, I took him daily to a friend's home to stay each day for his safety and get him after work.

I met with my friend Mark, a counselor, who helped me understood what I should do about this situation. As mentioned before, I wanted to leave but did not know how, and was concerned about legal repercussions. He sat with me for a very long time and was very passionate about this abusive situation. I took notes and vowed to myself to do everything possible what he told me to do. I was suffering greatly with the physical pain intensifying. And through all that I was not aware of the real injury been inflicted in my body. The doctors could not find out what was wrong and it appeared I was left to die. The pain had intensified to the point when I felt I would not live, but I knew I had to leave. I felt every day was my last day.

Then the abuse was carried to a new level—grandstanding. Grandstanding is public war and humiliation, planned and executed effectively by the enemy—the abuser. It can be through these dark times you realized that even the people you thought were your enemies can be a savior to you and others. During his last grandstanding, this lady stood up for us so powerfully to defend us that the darkness instantly became light—instantly and literally. Instantly, all the fears and darkness lifted from me, and I felt a very heavy presence and weight removed from my entire being.

And immediately, right there this marriage and all its baggage came to an abrupt end. I felt free from every depression, sorrow, and fear of any consequences of my future actions to be free and leave him behind, by himself. I knew instantly what my plans were must be implemented quickly and without fear.

EYE WITNESSES

To say the darkness literally lifted, is saying that the darkness physically and spiritually lifted, and all who witnessed the grandstanding also saw what I saw. The abuser was very shocked, got angry and walked away only about fifteen feet away from us. He angrily grabbed a chair, sat, and growled at us. Where he sat was a well-lit place. However, when he got there, instantly that place became darkened, almost black. A physical darkness came over him and all were shocked, horrified, and angry at the same time, because the true character of the man was then revealed for all to see.

Not everyone who witnessed this incident actually came to the terms and the realization that it did happened. I believe they were too horrified to put in words what they actually saw. Those who had the authority and power to do something, were standing beside him and close by at the time of the incident chose to say, "We saw nothing, we heard nothing." Others came to the shocking realization of how much we were suffering. Immediately, one of the leaders mourned deeply. She wept bitterly and encouraged me to leave quickly.

It is inconceivable at times to think how much injury an individual can heap on others. In your experiences it is also correct to say that those individuals who chose to ignore what was happening to you may have no credibility with you on any level. The very people who are in position of authority to come to your defense chose not to.

People are often afraid of what they see, of what they do not understand and some do not care. Most people who witnessed your humiliations have also suffered these kinds and worse. So why do they not all seem to groan in their body and soul against your suffering?

Most abused individuals are not healed, nor allowed themselves to heal completely. Most have not started their process of healing. Many blamed themselves for their own sufferings, never learned from them, and consequently blame you for yours.

Abusers want you to be publicly humiliated to show others that this is what you have brought them to as though you are responsible for their behavior. It is a control tactic used as a last resort to put you under their control to make you most subjugated to their every whim. According to the abuser's thinking, publicly humiliating you should cause you to be too embarrassed to speak up in your own defense, and if you do the abuser will use it to prove to the witnesses that you are insolent constantly as their reason for their behavior toward you.

Abusers want communities, leaders, your circle of friends, and family to fear them, and through public humiliation they are demanding from you certain responses to verify their cruelties. This tactic of fear can be very compelling depending on the heart of the individuals who are witnessing this. The abuser is trying to prove to you the victim that no one cares for you to step in your dark circle to stand on your behalf.

Witnesses to your Egypt clearly see the strain of oppression you are under but some will not dare step in. Their excuses are:

(1) They blamed you for the abuser's cruel behavior. They rationalize that for the abuser to come out in public like this you must have provoked this somehow.
(2) They simply do not care.
(3) They are afraid of what will happen to you later when alone with the abuser if they intervene.
(4) They do not understand their own authority and power over the abuser. They do not understand that they are literally their brother's keepers. Meaning—they can be and will be held responsible for the extent of your suffering that they were made aware of and allowed to continue for another minute while in their presence.
(5) They fear they could be excommunicated from the leader who may be the abuser, or from the company or community.
(6) Fear that exudes from the abuser affects witnesses so powerfully that it nullifies their brain and spirit crippling them from doing anything. Some horrible things we see in life can have crippling effects on us traumatizing us for life, making us unable to react rationally to situations normally we would not ignore.

People have different ideas of what you should and not do in this case. Only you know what will make you and your children safe. Staying focus on your goals is paramount. Stay focus quietly. Getting help quickly and quietly will save you and your children years of sorrow and pain later.

Clearly the abuser is out of control. It is a last desperate attempt to make you putty in their hands, to crush your spirit beyond recovery of self-worth. Immediately after this incident the abuser appeared elated and confused because of the intervention, and at the same time angry but did not know what to do with his newfound perceived power.

That day my son had left for youth camp for weeks and would not be exposed to the abuser. I prayed quietly with my whole being for my protection on the way home. On the highway the abuser tried several times to suddenly swerve the vehicle into other traffic to kill me but the steering wheel would not move. He tried to suddenly stop the car in high speed traffic but got frustrated when the car kept going straight in our lane and he could not control the speed and the car. I quietly thanked our Heavenly Father for such intense love and protection.

I made sure my son will be absent all summer with fun-packed long distance travel with youth camps, cadet camps with no opportunity for the abuser to hurt him. During this time I was able to obtain another part time job, and here too he tried to stalk me. The manager here became afraid and she kept closing the office earlier each night for fear the abuser may hurt them too.

REDIRECT YOUR FOCUS

Pharaoh was very intent on keeping the slaves more brutally enslaved. Our Creator was extremely, intensely focused on delivering the multitude of slaves at all cost. Each time Pharaoh promised to release them he would again change his mind and became more intent on killing them with increased abuse and heavy workload.

Moses several times tried to redirect their focus on the Creator, and how to regain and maintain their dignity and freedom. They were extremely discouraged and would have given up had he not stood in their dark world to intercede and help them. Now in their darkness He wants to give them hope by reminding them that because they cried out to their Creator they had and still have a Savior who will deliver them.

This may happen to you in your environment. It is through these times you may feel you are at your weakest, but you are at your strongest. Redirect your focus and pour your heart out to our Creator completely.

Redirecting your focus in these trying times is detrimental—a matter of life and death.

You must redirect your focus from the abuser to the Almighty for strength.

Through these dark times, I had difficulty sleeping, and frequently dreamt of fighting with fierce individuals. Each time I awake I felt as though I was wrestling with extremely strong individuals and my whole body felt warped and was experiencing intense pain.

I immediately chose to sleep in another room. This room was my sanctuary where my son and I would pray together to the Lord for help. This is where I would read the Savior's promises and mourn constantly for help, and the only room I could sleep without those dark dreadful dreams. While praying the abuser constantly insulted me during my prayers. I ignored the insults and prayed longer, and more fervently. During these dark times I constantly asked the Lord to explain to me what to do. I would cry feeling that He had forsaken me.

My body was experiencing intense pain day in and day out. I felt the darkness was surrounding and closing in on us and my child was afraid to sleep alone for fear of been hurt.

Before leaving the abuser I went to the doctor and tried to explain my pain. I told the doctor "I felt for certain our Creator had forsaken me. I never felt so much intense pain all at once for so long in all my life. He must have forsaken me." Immediately tears came to his eyes and he said, "No, He had not left you," and he continued to counsel me in explaining what was happening to me.

During this time before leaving, the Holy Spirit kept redirecting my focus on the suffering servant, YaHoshua, our Messiah. I tried to wave it off, thinking I already knew all about the story of His death. I found several books which illustrated the different individuals who witnessed His suffering and their reactions, and individuals who were directly responsible for His suffering.

The man from Cyrene who helped our Messiah carried His cross, knew nothing about Him, dared to show remorse for what was happening, and could have easily surmised that He may have deserved such cruelty. Yet he was moved with deep compassion and when the Roman soldiers saw his reaction they commanded him to help carried the cross. He needed not be compelled and was already willing to carry it.

In these times we must remember, stubbornly put in the forefront of our mind who is in complete control always and in everything and over everyone, certainly not the abuser. No one's ill concept of you can ever cause Him to ever give up control and authority in your life to any abuser.

COVER YOURSELF—A TIME OF RECKONING

While redirecting your focus you must cover yourself and your children. It was darkness for the multitude of slaves as Pharaoh now had gone as far as he could in hating our Creator by hurting His people. Death was surrounding them and they were afraid. They were instructed to stay in their homes and cover their door post with blood of lambs. This was to identify them as His, and to be untouched when the angel of death visit there. He was about to visit that place and whoever is not obedient to Him will suffer with the abusers.

It was now the Creator's turn to personally stop the abuser—completely, immediately, forever; slavery and its prosperity were to come to an abrupt bitter end.

A thick darkness came over Egypt, literally and physically, when the oppression upon the multitude of slaves had escalated to an extreme high. It was a fearful time for everyone, even to the oppressors. They were fearful because they do not understand what will happen next, and they could not perceive it. They knew they had done too much damage, gone too far, and that they were fighting against not just their victim but an invisible person who can snuff them out without instruments. *They were reduced to nothing but a certain fearful looking for judgments* ***(Hebrews 10:27).***

The powers of darkness in Egypt was about to have a rude awakening. They must be put under subjection in order to free all who cried for freedom.

This may be inconceivable to even think to equate this kind of suffering to an abused individual's environment. Yet it is no different. The purpose of oppression that created the darkness tightened around you the oppressed was intended for you to forget your Creator, who you were and can be, distress your children beyond recovery, and to put all your focus on them the oppressors. The abusers are fearful of what will happen to them, yet they cannot stop themselves from abusing.

Prejudice, discrimination, hatred, etc., many would say are the active forces in an abusive situation. But we know better. It does not matter what the nationality or color of your neighbor, who you marry, engaged to, is dating, or is associated with. When they decide to enforce an oppressive attitude and behavior toward you it is not about fear. They are fearful of you been a success because they have nothing to offer you. They will sometimes instigate violence in others against you through lies and deceptions to hurt and possibly kill you. Then you will learn that the motivator of abuse and oppression are neither the color of your skin, your economic situation, nor your nationality.

They may use these as excuses to hate you but are only smokescreens to hide their deep fears. Fear is the motivator of abuse and oppression. To cause someone to be afraid is to prove to themselves, the abusers, of their own illusions of superiority generated and propelled by their own fears.

You might become successful in fulfilling your own life goals which are different from the abuser's goals. The transitions in your life could change very quickly where they will benefit, but they do not see it and only fear being left out.

They do not care if their own families, neighbors, countries, would benefit from your success. To keep their life "as is," abuses are sometimes used to maintain that control. Even if they claim they are religious people our Heavenly Father will sift them out and expose them for what they really are.

When YaHoshua said, **"Whom the Son has set free is free indeed,"** does not mean abuse and other forms of oppression will not happen, because evil still exists today. This freedom gives you and your children options to not be held prisoners to any forms of abuse; to be more educated about your Creator, yourself, your environment; and to explore opportunities to improve your life to help others.

When our mind is focusing on who the rightful authority is in our lives, we will not allow ourselves to sink so low to transfer all adoration to another human who have no love for themselves and others to inflict hurt on you and your children.

Abuse is very offensive and people often believe that it is limited to physical violence. When we are treacherous with others through any forms of abuse these are extremely offensive to the soul and to our Creator.

Webster's dictionary defines:

Offense: *n. transgression, sin, insult, wrong, resentment, position or movement or attack.*

Offense is not limited to only the intended victim. Everyone in society is affected by this. Families are hurt, friends are hurt, people inside and outside your circle of belonging are hurt, whether they are directly or indirectly involved they are also hurt. Knowing how loving, patient, and kind our true Creator is, we will be free to take a stand against all that is offensive to our lives. Yahoshua said, *"I did not give you the spirit of fear, but the right to call me father."(**Romans 8:15**)* No one in this green earth has been given the authority to cause you to fear and to live in fear.

The powers of darkness in your world is about to be expelled and they knew it. That is why they intensified their persecution against you; to cause you to lose yourself and to be destroyed with them. Covering yourself and your children is very important. I prayed often with my son, anointing him and asked our Savior to shield us from injuries, guard our minds, health and to remember His promises to deliver us and bring us to His prosperity for us.

Make sure you make it right with Him and constantly redirect your children's focus to Him each day. I remind my son constantly of who our Savior is and how much He loves him, and of the dreams He gave me of reassurances of our deliverance. He never showed me how we would escape; only that He will deliver us, we will be out and will be happy, and the abuser will be dealt with.

It was never our Savior's intention for us to live in dreams. They are only of hope and directions to guide us back to the right path to continue in it. As long as our paths for deliverance are blocked it would be very difficult to focus on correct principles and instructions for healthy growth.

It is when you leave you will be able to understand your dreams, and be rightly educated and walk in His instructions.

Make sure that He is in everything you do to escape. It is not by your own power, but by His words and power you will have deliverance.

While my son was away for weeks after I was calm, very quiet and intensely focused on doing what I must, and so was he. The abuser was most pleased of the affects he thought he had generated in his own environment, supposedly under his control, and was smiling always.

A few days after this public humiliation, when asked why such cruel behavior, the response was, "All you have to do was be obedient and it would not have happened." Yet, it happened without provocation. Neither will they ever take responsibility for their actions. Abusers know that they are not worth answering. In any normal conversation with abusers when asked what would they do if they were the ones to be abused; instantly the answer: "No one in their right mind should put up with such nonsense."

Abusers know that their time is about to be up. They have done everything evil they could to you, and also know that if it was them in this situation they would be gone already! It is dangerous to them when you are staying focused. On what you could be doing they cannot tell, but they know they are causing you to endure more than humanly possible. The Heavenly Father is most powerful in shielding you while expediting His plans in delivering you and your children from the enemy's territory. They may see the children staying close and affectionate to you and not them. This may anger them more but in reality that is not your problem. Then they find other ways of getting even with you. You cannot always avoid it from happening, but you can guard yourself from losing focus on what to do. You must do all you can to protect the children and others when possible. The abuser's anger was never about you or anyone else but regaining perceived control they never had and lost, and want you to redirect your focus on them.

My friend Marco shared his story: During his time of focusing, while enjoying reading a good story to six year old his daughter, Branca, he prayed and to continue with what he needed to do making sure his daughter was safe and would not lose her mind. The abuser, his wife, sat and watched them with intense anger, sadness, and suspicion. Then she blurted out to him in despair, "I know you are leaving me." He saw her face, anger, and fear emanating all at once, heard her words and chose not to answer. His daughter immediately became afraid and pulled closer under his arm for safety. He held her close, continued to read to her, prayed, and showed her love, regardless.

In an abusive home, the abuser may stay around to make sure they know everything you are doing to have knowledge of your activities and to guarantee control over you. If they cannot stay around they will cause you such pain that you will not attempt escape.

Other cycles of rage may simultaneously begin. The abuser may continue to on a more frequent and fierce manner censor the children's every move in the attempt to destroy their mind. And they may be pointed out to you. Defend your children at all cost. Do not allow the abuser to cause you to hate them. If you do, you are becoming an abuser to your children and placing your children in great peril. Be determined not to allow this abuser to cause you to hate any children. They are in a home with an abuser, they will not act so normal due to the great distress heaped on them, and you must do your best to guard them, body, mind, and soul.

Friends were determined against the abuser's anger to now accelerate their help for us. Friends who increasingly dare to speak up to him against his behavior in our defense. After a while he did not like it anymore. He would speak very dark language to them in the attempt to frighten them. They did not back off, but rather accelerated their actions of care in more quiet and effective ways to help us and they did.

Another crisis occurred and because we only had one vehicle, this was easy for the abuser to effectively become offensive. I had to commute to work in another city one and half hours from our home and where my son's school was close by. He suddenly without warning decided he will not drive us. I confided in a friend about this who connected us to someone who commute daily to the city and worked only a few buildings from my son's school. This kind young man drove us there directly to his work, my son would walk over to school and I take the transit to work. After work we would both meet him at his workplace and get a ride home.

A few weeks of this and the abuser became angry. Perhaps his conscience was bothering him, I do not know, but he decided he will drive us. When doing this he was able to obtain job in the city. Another change of heart, he refused to drive us without any reason.

This was after we had moved to our new home. I noticed my neighbor beside us leaves every morning for work. After speaking to his wife I learned he commutes to the same city every morning along the same route as my child's school. They agreed my son and I could go with him each morning. At this time my other friend was working the night shift and could not take us. This nice neighbor drove us every morning and return home with him. He did this for months. Again the abuser was angry.

One of the first obvious signs of action/motive from an abuser is to destroy the victim's self-worth to bring them down to their level, to cause them to doubt themselves, their connection with their Creator, their value and true purpose, and to give up trying to be successful. There is nothing in them to give hope to the victim, and only escalate to other forms of abuse if not stopped from the onset.

This does not mean you must leave the abuser. Some people can cope with such displaced personality, ill temperament, and evil dispositions. However, you know better. These are dark times hard to deal with. It will not get better.

Violence does beat down the victim's self-worth until there is virtually no self and worth left. It is designed to destroy you.

Chapter thirteen

HELP IN STAYING FOCUSED

The experience that YaHoshua endured gave me courage to stay focused. At Herod's Hall, during YaHoshua's suffering inflicted by Herod, the crafty and his soldiers; His focus was intense under extreme cruel attacks of the enemy; because it was inflicted on Him all at once. What caused Him to be so focused, to not use His power to deliver Himself? What strengthened Him to have such strong resolve during such vicious attacks?

He knew it was the plan of the enemy prophesied to inflict on Him the most unjust hurt for our sins, and our lives have being weighed in the balance and there would be no justice for us if He had not endured. With such intense love for us and our children while facing such trials He knew our lives were at stake, and we will need to call on Him for help very soon.

While reading this book, my prayers for help to stay focused on Him were answered. I learned how to ignore the abuser and through all the avalanches of verbal abuse I was able to concentrate on YaHoshua's own focus. In Herod's Hall His abusers were very afraid of Him. At first they hated and tortured Him intensely. Yet He never answered them. They wondered why, what intense powers He may possess not yet displayed. What revenge could He possibly be reserving for them why He chose not to respond? They became more afraid of Him and because of that fear of losing control and power over this man if left to live, they chose to kill Him. Fear and hatred were two of the main reasons in the last episodes of their mistreatment of Him on Earth as a man, yet He died for other reasons.

In my time of darkness I chose to focus on His focus; because my attention was been constantly propelled into the self-centeredness of the abuser, always focusing on why the abuser was doing and saying this and that, and what the abuser meant. I desperately needed help from the Almighty for our safety.

When we are constantly focusing on abusers they get all the attention which fuels their ego and all our energy is drained while focusing on how to appease them as if they deserve it. The abuser was not worth any more of my focus and I refused to acknowledge and answer to any of his bellowed abuses. I focused my attention on my relationship with the Heavenly Father and on my son to help keep him stable, and the list of things my friend Mark suggested. Every task appeared to be time sensitive to be done for our survival to be accomplished urgently in preparation to leave and to re-establish ourselves afterward. Every contact must be made and each task must be done on time to accomplish my goals to leave.

Trying to appease the abuser is living in fear. This attempt is not out of love for life but out of fear that the abuser will lose control and hurt us and our children. It is a blame game we inflict on ourselves constantly judging, critiquing, and demeaning ourselves, our energy is constantly fueled by fear and self-blame. Its purpose is distracting you from more important things to do.

Understanding that we cannot control situations around us is very beneficial. The mind of people can neither be controlled nor predicted. Always focusing on what and why the abuser will do next is a total waste of time, and we are dismissing the abusers' responsibility for their own actions and consequences, and our own responsibility in using our own focus to better our lives.

The abusers are fearful when you are not answering them. They are afraid of what it is they cannot know about you to keep controlling you.

When we are afraid we are given the impression that the abuser knows everything about us. Even though the abuser is not with us 24/7, we believe that whatever we think and want to act on is already known. The abuser wants you to think that they have total knowledge and control over you. This is farthest from the truth. They want to know everything about you to control you and through mistreatment you will somehow blurt out all your plans for freedom and they will block you. Whether it is said to the abuser or others, the truth is that they cannot be trusted and will put you in jeopardy.

M.Scott Peck, MD in his book *The Road Less Traveled, the "risk of independence"*:

"Such major changes, such leaps into independence and self-determination, are painful enormously at any age and require supreme courage, yet they are not infrequent results of psychotherapy. Indeed, because of the enormity of the risks involved, they often require psychotherapy for their accomplishment, not because therapy diminishes the risk but because it supports and teaches courage."

http://www.ignaciodarnaude.com/espiritualismo/Peck,M.Scott,The%20road%20less%20traveled-1.pdf

Escaping from an abusive situation requires deep reflections of yourself, of those who depend on you, and of your situation. It does not come without fears. Counseling from someone you trust will definitely boost your courage to succeed. This courage you thought you never had will resurface and you will learn new ones, despite the risks of falling apart.

Chapter fourteen

THE DEVIL TREMBLES AT YOUR CALL FOR HELP

Moses in Egypt encouraged the oppressed people to stand firm and not be afraid. Most were terrified of the idea of leaving because they could not fathom the possibility of a better place, a better life ahead for them, somewhere, or that someone understood and cared, and were extremely frustrated to have the energy to comprehend it. They feared greatly that Pharaoh might change his mind again as he frequently did and send his army to block and possibly kill them for leaving him.

As Marco's wife, the abuser, accelerated her attacks against Marco and his daughter, Branca, she became more conscious of the fact that people will become more aware, and possibly become involved. She attempted to control them by interrupting all their interactions with people, even though they were not about her. It was an attempt to isolate his daughter and to prove Marco a liar. As a result of her behavior people became suspicious and began to ask questions. And he began to talk.

She next tried to isolate him more by demanding he does not speak on the phone with anyone, and attempted to screen his calls, and to switch authority of the phone account over to herself without his knowledge.

The abuser in your life may do all that, and perhaps in more threatening manner. It is a stand the abuser is taking to isolate you from everyone. If they are successful then you and your children will officially become their prisoner of war. You will be more isolated, abused, and no one will ever know you are suffering, because no one is allowed to talk with you.

It takes people of great courage to step up to the plate for you and stand firm in helping you. They need not be police officers, lawyers, or pastors, but simply people of great valor, people who are deeply moved with righteous indignation and recognize the work of the enemy in conduct and temperaments, people who are not afraid to stand and fight the enemy for you. The fight I am speaking of here is not a physical battle unless it is to subdue the enemy in your defense. It is warfare on higher and deeper levels that you the abused do not have strength for.

Many spouses of such people will not want their spouses to take such position of authority. They often rationalize all the negatives of why such victims are abused, and the possibility of their spouse being endangered been involved. Been involved does not mean violence, or to be afraid of the repercussions of doing right.

The main focus of abusers when they take their abuse to the open is to ascertain the weaknesses of people in communities: how the men and women they perceive have no backbone would dare interfere with their conduct. They are actually testing their playing field to see how far they can go. And if at all possible they would physically abuse you in front of the whole town, cut you in pieces and simply walk off. Because to them the community is discerning that you the victim deserve it, but more profoundly, they the abusers are in total control. Does this not give authority for legions of demons to be released in that neighborhood influencing others to abuse? And who is to say will not be the next victim.

Abusers during or after their grandstanding against you, may perceive they have new power to escalate their abuse to new levels, but not sure how because no one stopped them. Then the abuse against you may escalate in most violent ways possible.

Another reason the devil trembles at your call for help is the fact that our Creator does answer your call through people who do not know you. It is important to recognize these clues He gives you to escape your Egypt. Once a gentleman whom I never met greeted me, looked at me and said, "Get out of it. Do not stay in it. Run for your life." I had not said a word to him about anything, nor knew each other and I understood what he meant.

Another visiting pastor from another state preached at another church, who I had not spoken to. You will be amazed at how much our Heavenly Father show people who fear Him, things we the abused consider dark secrets, are not secrets to Him. "*Whatever is in darkness will come to light, and be sure your sins will find you out. He will do nothing but reveal his secrets unto his servants.*

Hebrews 4:12 The New English Bible: "*The word of God is alive and active. It cuts more keenly than any two-edged sword, piercing as far as the place where life and spirit, joints and marrow divide. It sifts the purposes and thoughts of the heart. There is nothing in creation that can hide from him; everything lies naked and exposed to the eyes of the One with whom we have to reckon.*"

In the midst of his sermon against abuse he looked directly at the abuser and exclaimed, "There are some who come to church with two piece suits, looking nice and regal, but at home you are nothing but a terror to your wife and kids. But it *will all end soon*!" Abuse is not okay with our Heavenly Father. The abuser was most quiet and unhappy.

It is the Word of the Father that will cause the enemy to tremble at your feeble cry to Him for help.

When He is allowing your dark secret to come out do not be afraid, He had sifted the abuser's heart and had seen all the evil they are aware and not aware of that exist in them He is preparing a way of escape for you, re-establishing joy, hope, and His authority and power in your life, and teaching you that the abuser had no rightful authority nor power over you. Their assumed authority and power is now over, never existed, and never to be re-established. He is also putting them on notice that He will destroy them if they do not stop their behavior. However, even if they repent does not mean they are genuine in their repentance to be good for you later.

Chapter fifteen

HELP TO CROSS

Recognizing your need of help to cross requires a heart of thankfulness. As awful your present environment may be it is important to be thankful to the Creator who brought you to this point in recognizing where you need help and cannot cross on your own, and not everyone in your situation can ask for help to get out. Many victims of abuse may recognize they need help but when the opportunity comes they are afraid to cross their Red Sea. To them the challenges seem more terrifying than their current situation.

When you are wholeheartedly thankful for future opportunities to light as much candles as you want, you will not want to stay. You know this Red Sea—a way out, must be parted for you. But only you can make that first step in allowing it to part, instantly.

This Red Sea is your friend, your wake-up call when you look beyond yourself and your place of darkness and realize what it is. At this point the soul must cry out with every cell in your body in union with voice realizing you must leave.

It is your friend when you reach out and ask for help to assess your situation and whatever is left of your dignity and your possibilities of recognizing again who you were and what has happened to you and the children. You may remember your original goals to succeed and start to crave those opportunities missed.

It is your friend when you choose to be still and focus on the necessities of preparation without caring the abuser may be watching; continue collecting important documents and correct information and begin the process of your freedom. Speak to people for help; lawyers, police officers, your boss, friends, strangers, doctor, a caring religious leader, real estate agent, etc. You will be surprised these individuals can be great sources of help. They may even share some of their experiences with you as hope for your circumstances.

Sift through them and see what will work for you. You may need to do it alone without the children knowing depending on their age and maturity. Or you can plan it with them, you decide. Continue to reassess where you are now compare to where you should really be. Calmly and quietly do what you must in your preparation to leave, and muster all the support you need. You are preparing to leave from a dark place to the unknown. But in the unknown you will be able to light as much candles as you want, freedom to create your own styles, grow your own flowers, reset, restore, and re-establish true values.

Even with these help available you may fear going it alone and look at your Egypt—abusive home, and may compare it against the unknown—the Red Sea your way of escape opened up.

Looking at your Red Sea, you may perceive no one else in the water. No one is swimming merrily or water skiing, boating, sailing—no one. The waters may appear too difficult to swim in and you feel you lack the skills to make it across.

It may appear to be barren land that stretches for thousands of miles, no relief in sight or water to refresh the soul to wash the wounds of the high heaped on debris of abuse. No trees in sight to represent shade or shelter for security to rest on.

The ground may appear too difficult to walk on, no grass to soften the bruised heels of humanity. Worst of all we see no one there in hope of having someone to talk with to help make the journey through more bearable and shorter than it really is.

You feel this way because you believe you are all alone, and that no one else could possibly be experiencing this horrible thing. You feel a sense of loneliness thinking the people in your life do not really care why they did not intervene when you expected. Surely they must have seen or suspect something. It appear to be a lonely road because you keep it all to yourself due to the constant degradation and humiliation you are experiencing and are afraid also for fear of the insults and discouragements you may experience along the way.

Looking back on the shore of your Egypt, or the edge of the barren land where you are now seemed a strange paradox. It may appear to be a broken patch of land on broken fortresses with breached walls. It may look green as the result of your hard work to appear to others outside everything is okay. This place of wreckage is an assumed home. The roof and walls are there in tact but are not secure. The windows are shattered because of the assumption that everyone knows the lies heaped on about the victims. So there is no security, no beauty as there is no peace, no words of cheer exist as they are never guaranteed.

In your decision to leave you will experience feelings of anxiety, terror, excitement, fear of the unknown and the feelings of unease in leaving this place are expected.

Looking now at your Red Sea, overwhelming feelings of guilt can set in. When you think of the weight of responsibilities heaped on you with the gravity of the situation, you may feel compelled to stay. And due to the duration of your time in the abusive environment it may feel almost criminal to leave. You could see from the experiences of others that this is neither the way to live or die. You do not want to die and have your bones buried in this place. Worst of all your family members and friends will only remember you for what you endured, why you decided to stay in it, what your life could have been had you left and tried to improve your life.

But the critical decision must be made; should you leave, or stay and put you and your children's lives at risk. Staying is to continue living in constant degradation of body, mind, and soul which need to be correctly nurtured constantly. This indeed is a '*dry place*' because of no true source of proper nutrients. What appear to be sources of nutrients are poisoned with ill content. The body not only needs physical food to grow but also peace of mind that nourishes the soul to prosper.

One of my deepest fears was if I was to die in this place, what would happen to my son. He was too young to decide where to stay. No one would know where they are, because family and friends were blocked from us. I prayed constantly, a "heart rendering" cry begging our Heavenly Father to let me live long enough to see him grow up and able to care for himself in every way.

I reasoned it was better to leave with him, giving him a chance to live and be free to experience the goodness of our Creator far away from an abusive home and the abuser. I wanted him to know he can live a better quality life without growing up in abuse; his heart can be free to laugh, be peaceful, learn, love, and be loved, be prosperous, connect with family and friends, and know that he is loved and can be cared for if I was to die before he could care for himself.

Years before someone gave me the option of protecting my son and how to safely leave the onslaught of the enemy. My son and I used that information in formulating our own plan.

Abusers are angry, and mostly afraid of your confidence in yourself and your Creator to do what only you can do for yourself. They neither care nor have skills to help you to be happy.

For some time this became our plan and we kept that secret for dear life. With my part-time job restored I was able to save enough money, make arrangements to place him in the dormitory school.

While speaking with my friend Mark, I made a list of things I must do to get out correctly and safely. I was able to understand the extent of the various abuses we endured and how to stop them immediately without fear.

I understood how to confidentially secure all legal documentations and communications before and after leaving for our protection; how to obtain police assistance if need be at that time of leaving, and if not go to a shelter where we would be safe. I never had the freedom and space to properly re-document and complete everything for our future, but in the initial contact with certain companies in starting the changes they understood what I was experiencing and were very helpful in keeping the process very confidential for our protection and knew what to do in the event I did not live.

I communicated with the dormitory school and he was placed there, safe far from the abuser until I could leave. The court had already given me emergency custody over my son. The abuser became angry and tried to interrupt my son's transition for safety. The school staff understood my son's plight and did not help the abuser. He could not succeed, eventually he gave up. Here at the dormitory school he was free to breathe, was counseled daily for the first year, healed, be himself, reconnect with family, make new friends, and succeed.

It may be at this point some victims may consider staying now the child is safely away, and how possibly they could cope with the abuser. Bad idea! Do not assume that the calmness in your home between episodes of abuse is any promise for a better life.

Living in subjugation to an abuser is to be totally controlled by them keeping you in a box with no available opportunities to do well, blocking your access to full sunshine in fulfilling your own responsibilities to grow.

These rays of sunshine are blocked because of the abuser's controlling behavior, dictating what and when to think, and wanting to make choices for you.

Abusers are like continuous dark clouds overshadowing the lives of their victims, blocking every sunray. Even though the sun is shining and there are better ways to live, the oppressor may be aware of that but does not want you to see this; because their soul is darkened by evil thoughts constantly.

Yet the soul of the abused will always cry out, groping for some rays of hope, deliverance, love, and freedom. If none of these are found the abused may give up, identify with the abuser through total submissive, adopt a masochist attitude, or die. This death is a result of abuse and the intense frustration due to lack of sunrays to the soul that manifests in the body as various kinds of illnesses.

The fear to leave can be crippling to oneself and to others who depend on you. If you are too fearful to move on the children will know and lose heart because they see you doing nothing.

While teetering with the idea of leaving and focusing only on your health, more seriously consider the health of the children as detrimental. They are often confused in this type of situation and often may act out in ways unfamiliar to us. Monitor their health closely. Chronic emotional distress can cause their health to suffer. Constantly monitor their progress in school. Talk often with them about what hurt them, allow them avenues to talk it out with you, family, trusted friends, family doctor, and a counselor if possible.

When you empathize with the children's feelings it will boost their confidence and keep them stable regardless of their fears.

Because they let you know in no uncertain terms that they have reached their limits in coping, you can plan with them.

If the abused parent is having difficulties empathizing with the child's sorrow to leave, get help from others—medical professionals, counselors, family or friends. It is important to understand what the child is trying to say and to correctly discern the dangers the child faces each day living with and been alone with the abuser.

When the parent sees the danger and chose to do nothing, the child is left alone to carry a burden for the rest of his/her natural life. This burden is more entrenched and entwined than a ball of elastic bands or an entangled electrical circuitry. Each wires appear to have no beginning and no end, and the longer the child carries that burden alone, the more it becomes part of the neurological pathways been developed; with each synapses distressed and not able to recognize/identify with the neurotransmitters each negative emotions and the continuous release of stress hormones triggers to the brain to release.

The brain as a result of long-term exposure to abuse is forced to accept this as "normal" altering its healthy processes to either adapt or shut down. The results can be: breakdown in the immune system affecting the blood's ability to process nutrients from food, and the breakdown of other vital organs, neurological disorders, and even death itself.

You are preparing to leave when you realize that any place is better than where you are now. You and your children are blocked of every opportunity to succeed, and all the doors you knocked on for jobs and friendships were not heard.

It is not because you were not heard, but you lived in a dark place that cast a shadow on you, robbing you of your inner beauty that should shine outward, but did not. You were not ready and it was not the right time to shine as your candle would continuously be doused with the vacuum air of continuous despair.

The victims of abuse are rose plants hidden from the sun by the dark clouds of fear and distress. A rose plant with only the promise of rose, embedded in the rotten soil of malnutrition to body, mind, and soul.

You merely stayed alive because of scanty rays of sunlight which are the occasional display of love from outside influence—people who dare to show you love regardless of the dangers, who dare to step into your territory or war zone and speak up for you, and your children. Even though your friends may dare to correct the abuser, the dark clouds remain as the abuse may increase because the abuser is now embarrassed to be found out and somebody will be punished for it.

Others can lose heart if they see you are reluctant to step out of the abusive home. Their hopes for your deliverance and success are very high and attainable if only you will try. You know they will not come in your home and lift you out physically, but you must tell them you need help to leave and stay out. Your children will have no future staying behind in this hell with the abuser because their safety cannot be assured. All this they will mourn.

Many individuals may tell you stay and cope—for their own fears of you leaving and possibly not succeeding. Their own fears are more deep rooted in their attempt in transferring them to you; fearing you leaving and becoming successful as they see your passion for life and the desire for the opportunities to explore and develop them. Some are not aware of help you could get in the community to succeed and will implore you to stay, indicating; "This is the only shelter and life you may ever have," according to their narrow minds. Some are simply wicked in their attempts to make you feel totally responsible for your situation insisting you stay. But there is no reprieve for any marriage or relationships where there exist any kinds of abuse. Some are experiencing their own hell in their "marriage/intimate relationship" and hate to see you have the audacity wanting to leave.

You long for a life of good quality—a life of dignity, peace and strength that only our Creator can give. Abuse may increase at this point as the enemy see that you are escaping their territory. It will work in the mind of the abuser to force you to stay by heaping on you more abuse. This is an attempt to cripple you, to cause you to be confused and lose focus. The abuser is saying that "I need someone to constantly abuse, to transfer all my pain unto, to let out steam on, someone to blame for my day's frustration, someone to control . . ." Take a stand, even if only in your mind, that you and your children are precious. You have been enslaved financially, emotionally, physically, and spiritually, and perhaps sexually been abused for too long. However long it may have being was too long.

Their scanty displays of affection and the material things gave you false hope and false sense of security and it became the only existence you knew for a while. You look at the physical things you may have accumulated over the years and may ask yourself, "How can I leave them behind and possibly start over again?" What about my job if I must relocate? What about the assets we accumulated together?

At your Red Sea you continue to experience new fears, stresses, and anxieties. You know you need these material things but can you afford to purchase new ones. You may feel if you leave them behind they must be replaced all at once to set up another home quickly and adequately. These things may have been a source of "comfort" at one time. Now they seem a necessity and a burden because you cannot see the possibility of safely moving them out nor replacing them, and fearful of been seen by the abuser.

These things may now seem to have no real future value, and your willingness to walk away from them can bring healing and peace. This may not be what you choose, but if trying to retrieve them will endanger you, remember—*things are replaceable. You and your children are not.*

I became more determined to leave and during this time I was fiercely protective of myself in every way because of how I felt I refused to eat or drink anything in the home. I could not tell my son because he would be greatly distressed. And I worked more quickly in preparing to leave. I know my son was very worried for my safety and I reassured him as often as possible, yet I knew this Egypt—his past home is not where I want him to return to see me.

Chapter sixteen

YOU NEED AN ARMY

The multitude of slaves had to escape, but how. They could easily pack their bags, pots and pans, and their animals and say, "We are leaving." However, neither was it conceivable to leave the enemy territory peacefully and quietly, nor would it be safe.

You may be thinking escaping your Egypt seem more difficult than staying; or you may think you have enough will power to stay and make it work. Or you may feel dynamiting your way out will take a great feat. You will need an army for that.

Many years ago, at a huge conference a lady spoke of her ordeal been trapped in the Middle East. She was stuck with all her children, abandoned by her husband without any source of support for them, and was constantly harassed by the men in the community. They had no way of escape. One day she cried out to the Lord—"It will take an army to get us out of here. Lord, please provide for us an army." To her it was an impossible prayer, but a last resort for her. Would you know it that was exactly our Heavenly Father's plan! Saddam Hussein declared that *all Americans must leave*! It was her deliverance! They all had to leave to allow her and all her children to leave. If that was not deliverance, I do not know what is.

Maxine shared her story of been constantly assailed by her abusive husband. Nowhere was safe for her. He would constantly pursue her threatening to kill her. She could not live anywhere without fearing for her life. This abuser did not know he was been pursued by both police and our Creator's army surrounding him at the same time. One day during his pursuit of her he was stopped by police and arrested. How far will our Father allow an abuser to continue hurting you?

In 2 Kings 6:15--18 Elisha, when approached by his servant who was fearful of the army sent after them, prayed for our Creator to open his eyes, and his prayers were answered as the servant saw the army of Holy angels surrounding them.

The Israelites were fearful as they approached their Red Sea. How to cross they had no idea. Even if they could swim it was not possible with all their possessions, children, animals, and helping the elderly. Pharaoh and his army were directly behind them in full view, and the multitude of slaves appeared defenseless, *stuck between the devil and the deep blue sea.*

Our Creator immediately showed them they needed an army, and was exactly that for them.

Before the Red Sea experience, He was very merciful in keeping Pharaoh alive throughout the plagues and disasters. He had directed the multitude of slaves through another route with the single purpose of taking the people out of Egypt and leave Pharaoh to himself. However, Pharaoh realizing the route and supposed he would have the support of other nations to totally destroy the already weakened slaves, decided to pursue them. This was to the extreme. He could not leave well alone.

It was evident Pharaoh had gotten on our Creator's "last nerve," as we humans would term it, had past his limits and now was testing Him to the maximum. In Exodus 14:18-31,

He showed his extreme hate for abuse and toward abusers who will not stop regardless of numerous warnings.

He himself cannot endure abuse inflicted on anyone and here He was forced to show His terrible side as a result of the abuser's persistent behavior. His presence became a blockade between the multitude of slaves and the Egyptian army: in the form of extremely thick darkness; and light occurring simultaneously side by side at the same spot, yet not blending. Total darkness for the Egyptian army preventing them from seeing what He was doing for the people crossing the Red Sea, and light for the slaves who needed to escape through the Red Sea on dry land.

The multitude of slaves escaped successfully, and the darkness from Pharaoh's army was lifted. He pursued the slaves through what he perceived was a cave, on this road not made for him and his army but only for the multitude of slaves, where He ended the pursuit: out there in the Red Sea. The walls of water closed in on Pharaoh and he and all his army died out there.

The internet source for the ***Works of Josephus*** **is: Josephus, antiquities of the Jews, William Whiston, Translator (1737)—Antiquities of the Jews Book II**. In the writings of Josephus ben Matthias (Flavius)—this battlefield in the Red Sea—between God and the Egyptians was well defined: *"The Egyptians were not aware that they went into a road make for the* multitude of slaves, *and not for others; that this road was made for the deliverance of those in danger, but not for those that were earnest to make use of it for others' destruction."*

This He can do for you not on such a mass scale if not necessary; but deliverance the same. Many governmental policies have been changed to help oppressed people be free. He will cause the abuser to remain in darkness and confusion, while He gives you clear vision and purpose of direction to leave.

My son had left for about two weeks now, and during that time my health suffered more rapidly and the doctors could not find out the cause because they were not looking for anything out of the ordinary.

Many wicked individuals tried to berate me for the situation which only propelled me forward. Looking at their own misery why would I want to listen to them. I knew I was beautiful before this life and can be more beautiful after.

Your army may not be soldiers or police officers protecting you but He will empower friends in your life and even people you do not know to be an army for you and take a stand on your behalf, to encourage you and help expedite your escape.

A week before I left the abusive home, a group of people decided to pray together for my deliverance and my son's continuous protection. We often believe that we can go it alone; we do not need anyone's help. How on our Creator's green earth could I do that. I became so weak I could not pray anymore. I could not even formulate a plan and execute it to leave safely. I needed an army. My son was already out and I almost gave up hope of leaving safely.

An army He gave me. A lady I never had the chance to speak with, came to me and said; "Comgin, what is wrong? You do not look good. I watch you all the time, and you are walking too fast. You are about to fall apart. Tell me what is wrong," she had insisted. I could not speak, and all the resolve I thought I had to cope with all this trauma began to dissolve. And I began to cry. I tried to tell her but the words could not come. She comforted me and told me, "Tell me what you want us to do for you." I told her, "Please get a group of people together and pray for me and my son to leave." She agreed.

We often believe that we can go it alone, we do not need anyone's help. I was trying to go it alone. How on this green earth could I do that. I became so weak I could not pray anymore. I could not formulate a plan and execute it to leave properly. I needed an army.

This army was a group of prayer warriors. During those four days of my conversation with my friend, she had secretly gathered together certain individuals and they prayed for me and my son. I constantly prayed to the Creator for the opportunity to get out and He did.

That opportunity became available, and I saw physically before me a panoramic view of my Red Sea and all I had to do was to step in it and it would instantly part for me, like a physical path that was not there before that suddenly appeared and it was the correct path. After four days of my friends praying for me, I was out of there.

I instantly understood what it meant and that it was the only time of escape I had. I felt if I did not leave then I would never have another chance to leave alive, and that path may never reappear. I immediately called a couple whom I met who helped me to move only some items. These items were valuable items my child had made and what others had made for him. These were priceless and I encouraged him to keep them as reminders to be thankful. I regretted leaving other things behind especially his grand upright piano, but was pleased to be out. These things were stored at one of my friend's home.

When I left I took nothing for myself, left with only the clothes on my back. I left all furniture, my own clothes, dishes, books, plants, etc. All those clothes were dreadful reminders of who I was with, what happened to me when I wore them, and the smell was no longer appealing to me. The dishes reminded me of the constant hunger we experienced, the furniture, of who sat there and the painful events that came with them. We need the prayers of our friends.

We do a great disservice to our community, friends, counselors, and family, and our Creator when we try to go it alone. We are not only preventing Him from working through people who are willing, but also a great disservice to others who can be blessed in witnessing the result of their heartfelt cry to Him on your behalf. People need to see what He can do for you, how He has responded in your situation, even if all they could do was cry on your behalf.

Chapter seventeen

COVER ALL YOUR EXITS

Follow correctly all legal rules and secure your exits. Your exits are your leaving points from the abusive home/marriage/ situations and your entry points to and through your red sea. Although you may not have time to have everything worked out as planned before you leave, immediately after leaving make sure you enlist all wanted help in completing them with a sense of urgency to secure present and future safety.

Using help and advice given you, assess your plans carefully. Review them with someone who can be trusted in your situation, a lawyer, counselor, trusted family member, bank manager, insurance company, or a doctor. Continue research and put things in motion. Do what is necessary. Friends your family share may not be best to help, unless they express a heartfelt desire to do so. Ask them to help protect your privacy. My friends were very helpful in storing things for me and keeping my privacy.

Presence of abuse on such levels indicates the marriage is over if continued too long without help, and only escalate to other forms of violence.

When I finally left I could neither care nor grieve what and whom I left behind. I immediately completed changes to documentations on my life insurance where the abuser was a main beneficiary. After realizing what was happening to my body there is no way in this green earth he would get a dime from me. I also changed my will and eliminated him from it. My bank accounts had to be changed with added security to them. Many more legal documents had to be changed for me and my son. And I also disconnected the home phone in my name he had continued to enjoy after me leaving.

Through the initial court process I learned how to assign temporary trustee for my son until a permanent trustee/legal guardian was assigned in the event I did not live. At his new location staff members were aware of what was happening. They immediately responded and were determined to protect him in every way, including the privacy of his files from others who later tried to obtain information of our address to inform the abuser to inflict more harm to us. The school was a constant support for him and they understood very well what this involved

It was not important to me what people think of me and my actions, and took that giant leap of faith because our lives depended on it.

Your work place, educational institutions, recreational, or professional associations you are involved with that the abuser may know of, inform them of this situation to help you protect your privacy and possibly help you in the event of any attacks of the abuser.

Leaving an abusive home is not the same as agreeing to a temporary separation in resolving disagreement with help of counselors. In the case of disagreement the issues can be reconciled. An abusive situation is extremely hostile with the absence of all security, love, hope, and safety. The abuser has expressed to you in no uncertain terms they have only hate toward you. Their mind is extremely dark and you will never grow and bloom in this place of darkness they have created for themselves to involve you.

Abuse is neither the result of disagreement or misunderstanding. This is something too dark, deeply disturbing, cannot be comprehended, and its origin in the abuser cannot be accurately traced.

Now you have left you may be trying to understand the deep rooted cause of such behavior or what you may have done to cause such behavior.

You are not in a position to be the abuser's counselor. Trying to be their shrink will cause you to take on a burden too heavy to carry and you become the abuser's dead conscience been blamed for their every evil actions.

The Creator hates all forms of oppression. He hates to see the poor oppressing the poor. The poor—the abuser, is lacking creativity and imagination of how to love and grow. They cannot see beyond their own selves and want the world to be centered on them, are unbalanced and only evil result from their evil thinking. That centeredness blocks and limits your space for light and growth.

The other poor are the victims who have been gravitated in the darkness of the abuser's self-centeredness which has enveloped them and their light is forced to grow dim to eventually be put out permanently. It is an evil device and tactic the enemy employs through the minds of abusers to the victims in the attempt to create generations of darkness.

It is very shocking and most horrendous what the human soul is exposed to endure. Yet it is not of one's own strength they endure. Had it not been for the Heavenly Father's power it would have been extremely terrible where this evil would also occupy the victims' spirit, soul, and body completely had He allowed it to happen. The human soul is extremely fragile and can only endure so much distress, if any at all, and was not created for darkness and distress or it dies.

Chapter eighteen

PLACES OF REFUGE

In the Old Testament (Deuteronomy 19), places of refuge were for criminals, guilty or innocent, to escape; given a chance to live before their cases can be heard by the leaders.

Places of refuge are places and people you will meet through your Red Sea, and after. These can be employers, friends, shelters, strangers, and even your child's school.

The dormitory school was a place of refuge for my son in securing his safety before I could leave. There He was protected at all cost against the abuser and religious leaders from our communities who tried to aid the abuser in finding us to continue hurt on us.

My friend's home was a place of refuge along the path through our Red Sea. The abuser kept pursuing, but he could only come so far. He called all the people he thought I was in contact with.

He eventually called this home where I was. My friend's mom answered the phone and harshly reprimanded him for his behavior. He kept talking about a terrible incident where he injured my son; as though he was deeply sorrowful and at the same time requesting I was there they should send me back to him.

They were not moved by this because they too have had enough of his behavior and did not like him anymore. I listened happily to her harsh rebuke directed at him. She said, "Oh your wife is no longer there with you. Is that right? She left you. Oh sorry to hear that. That is too bad for you. Did I not tell you all these years to treat your wife and kid good? Did I not tell you? See there now you have no wife what you want me to do? I can't help you! You are on your own!"

Immediately her daughter took the phone and more harshly reprimanded him, "Don't you know what time of the night it is? Why are you calling us like this? Get off the phone!"

Before she could finish her last sentence he was gone, and never called again, even to this day. Don't we all need friends like that!

He called others and no one cooperated when asked of our whereabouts but also harshly reprimanded him for past cruel behaviors and demanded not to be contacted anymore. They too have had enough of his mistreatments to us and others and will not indulge the abuser. If you think that friends, family, and strangers do not feel your pain during your stay in your abusive home, think again. People are hurting and often feel powerless to do anything on your behalf. But when you take that giant leap of faith to leave, it empowers them to act on your behalf powerfully without regrets.

UNEXPECTED DETOURS

Frequently moving about with no permanent address is often not an option for some abused individuals. It is often a last resort in the hope of finding a place to call home. I was encouraged to relocate and reside close to my son's new location to give him the support needed, because he was too young at the time. I was not sure how I would do that with my two part-time jobs as the only sources of income to support both of us. My health was deteriorating more rapidly and I felt I would die soon. However, I was determined to finish sort out the legal processes quickly and was successful in obtaining emergency custody.

I remembered my aunt whom I told of our dilemma was taken aback by this to say the least. She was always kind and supportive to us and although she lived a great distance was a great source of emotional help. When I told her I left the abuser and still in the area she simply said, "It is not good to stay in the area because the abuser would come after you and harass you." I told her he was already doing that and I explained to her my work situations. While at my friend's home I realized that was true and should not remain there. My friend's home was offered to me permanently but it was a bit too close for comfort regarding the abuser and too far to help my son.

I decided after visiting my son to visit the shelter for information making it one trip to save on transportation costs. When I arrived I was too ill to walk up the stairs without help. They realized what was happening to me and tried to explain but I could not understand. I realized I was trying to live on sheer will power and blamed myself for everything happening in my environment and my life.

Fortunately for me I was in the right place to be helped. That night I could not return to my friend's home. I was too ill and was sent to the hospital's emergency department where they quickly determined my heart was too enlarged and my body contained nonbiological toxins at an extreme high level. I needed treatment immediately or I would not live.

For a while my son was fearful I would return to the abuser and needed much reassurance. He was reassured after the staff communicated with him that I was out and invited him to stay with me for the weekend. He came and realized we were completely removed from the abuser never to be reconnected. Afterward he began to heal.

Make no mistake our children feel what we are feeling. They have deep bowels of compassion for our plight and cannot relax until they know we are safe. They are expecting you to do your best leave and be safe, to provide a safe home for them to return to you. They need to come home to you, for holidays, weekends, and possibly permanently, until they are ready to be on their own. They need a safe place to heal and be restored, and they want you to provide it for them.

Knowing my physical illnesses caused me to realize my other limitations in solving my problems. I needed to stop for a while and rest, while gradually limiting my daily activities to avoid setbacks in my recovery. The staff at the shelter was extremely helpful in directing us to the right places for counseling and medical treatments.

Chapter nineteen

TRUE SHEPHERD—GUIDE FOR YOUR JOURNEY

Psalm *23:3—He restores my soul; He leads me in the paths of righteousness for His name's sake.*

Going through the crucibles of life is not easy. Your crucibles in an abusive home can be many things all equivalent to abuse. We cannot afford to use human reasoning alone to penetrate the walls of our Egypt. Our Creator's power is needed. It is easy to say, "Why me, why me, it should not be happening." And you are correct it should not be happening to anyone.

The very person we gave our heart, body, and time to seeks our life. Often times abused individuals believe if only they had tried harder the abuser would not have done this or that. They even want to blame themselves for the individual's temperament.

Through this intense anger I was experiencing, I often wondered what can I possibly learn, but I know the One who leads us out and will continue with us. I reflected on how much we had endured and how difficult it was to keep our focus.

We could not go through this journey alone. Concerns for our safety increased and we needed wisdom in who we speak with because many questions were asked to determine our new locations.

I could not understand how going through such intense dark times could my soul ever be restored. How could going through this dark path be paths of righteousness and why for His name's sake? The price YaHoshua, the Messiah paid for our freedom was extremely high, and He did not want to see us going through this alone.

He is very tenderhearted, patient with each of us and does not desire for any of us to be lost. ***First Peter 2:25*** *"You were straying like sheep, but now you have turned toward the Shepherd and Guardian of your souls."*

In our abusive homes we were been deceived by the enemy of our soul. Make no mistake; abuse is not to tell you are loved. It is telling you the absence of what you are getting—no love. And it is not coming any time soon. He knows your heart, your tireless effort to please the abuser, the true quality of life you desired, and your need for safety. You needed to be rescued for healing and restoration back to Him.

Work with Him here. Do what you know you must and He will cause things to fall in place.

Ezekiel 34:1—*"As a shepherd goes in search of his sheep when his flock is dispersed all around him, so I will go in search of my sheep and rescues them, no matter where they are scattered in dark and cloudy days."*

People of diaspora from all nations and tribes, are experiencing dark times, scattered all over the land, lost, abused, not belonging anywhere. So it is with abused individuals needing a place to belong. The past place of abuse is no longer in existence, because you cannot identify with the abuser. You do not belong there and you were not created to be abused because it was unnatural. He is the ultimate authority and power to break those evil chains of oppression and set you free.

He will use people with clean and caring hearts, even other people in positions of authority to help break those chains of oppression. I am always thankful for all such individuals including leaders who cared and counseled. I often reflected on my aunt's husband who is a pastor and wished with all my being all religious leaders were like him in character. His character has taught me over the years of what true leaders are to be to people, and his many encouragements to us during our times of recovery.

WHO IS YOUR SHEPHERD

Psalm 23:1—*The Lord is my Shepherd, I shall not be in want. 2. He makes me lie down in green pastures, he leads me beside quiet waters,*

In Joshua chapter 6, the Israelites came to an impasse. It was a literal wall which caused great distress to their soul. Besides they have not fully recovered from the shock of the Red Sea, and now what, another one to overcome. Their only way to live this one out was to follow instructions.

After leaving the oppressor, the situation may become intense, but you will get through it. Acknowledging the power and reason for your anger can give you a purpose to strive to fulfill.

When a spouse has been abusing you and/or your children in anyway, privately or publicly and you leave the abuser, that same demonic spirit will often work in the dark hearts of others, including leaders to continue on a wider and more powerful scale the abuse in every way to continue the hurt on you. It will try to attach itself onto you to prevent your escape. You must take a strong stand against this to rebuke it by getting help to quash it from the onset. Only YaHoshua, the true Messiah and His Word, can deliver you from it. Ask Him for help and He will help you.

Knowing who your shepherd is and why you left can save your life.

The first day of court would be held in the abuser's home town and I was not allowed to leave the shelter unless my safety was reassured. After verifying with my friend whom I just left that I would stay with them I was allowed to leave.

I attended court and a few strangers—friends of the abuser approached me afterward demanding I stopped the divorce proceedings and return to the abuser. In the court room they approached me and viciously demanded that I return to the abuser without any counseling and proof of his changed behaviour, nor any concern for my safety. They continued to threaten me with no regard for the judge and other court officers, of how much they would publicly humiliate me right there if I did not return to the abuser and how I am a disgrace. I will not be accountable to anyone who has no concern for my life, and I boldly and loudly continued to counteract each threat by publicly declaring my freedom to never return to the abuser. I told them I really do not care and continued to loudly make my declaration of freedom to never return. I have had enough of the abuser and these wicked people who do not care about anyone's safety. I was intensely angry and fighting for my son's life.

While the judge attempted to reprimand them for their cruelty towards me, I responded. I was very full and over-flowing with anger and grief. It was there in the court room I had really exploded. I turned around and a huge crowd was behind me in the court room with intense silence had stopped and was listening to this including my legal counselor standing outside her office door, and I saw my counselor signaled for everyone to listen. And I knew the people in the whole perimeter of that court room all heard me. There were judges, lawyers, police officers, counselors, and other clients. They all heard me and they all stood there and listened. I was shocked and intensely angry at the same time. My counselor smiled, quietly clapped her hands, and called me back in her office.

She congratulated me for standing up for my rights and gave me more counsels. His claims against me were not considered by the court as a result of this public humiliation toward me.

This is not the time to feel sorry for yourself in this fight for your life, the regaining of your dignity—whatever is left of it; and the good quality of life you so desperately long for you and your children and you will do all that is right to get it. Neither is it the time to rationalize the causes and ill effects of leaving an abusive home and the abuser. It is definitely not the time to even care about feeling sorry for leaving or care about assessing any damage. You are not in the damage control business at this time. Who cares if the abuser is hurting and angry, so are you. They must get over it and so must you. They do not have to like the message that you must be free, but they must get it.

Many people do not care about victims of abuse. Do not allow their threats to frighten you into submission and subjugation to any more forms of abuse. If they really were any good shepherds for anyone's soul they would not behave that way.

Our Creator does hate divorce. Divorce is not limited to marriage in obtaining the divorce certificate. It is a separation from good to bad, separation from His love, authority, and peace to our own way. Fortunately He is not limited to His own rules. His principles given to you are for your well-being to live harmoniously with others. He said, "Thou shalt not do murder." Yet, if that is what it takes to set you free, He will do it for you.

The Egyptian army was swallowed up in the Red Sea, and who can judge Him for that.

Abuse is not a private affair. Some wicked individuals would like you to think it is, because they do not want to bother with it, even when it permeates to their own circle where they can be made accountable.

Certain religious leaders wanted me to feel guilty for damaging the family unit when I chose to leave the abuser; "Children who are without fathers in their lives will come out to nothing good." These were their actual words, and they pierced my soul. Yet they were raised by mom only and no father.

My response to them was: "You do not know what my Creator had taken us from. Who are you to tell me my son will come out to nothing good? My son is hurting and he will heal with His help. Who do you think you are? Shut up! You have no idea what we were experiencing and how He took us out. You do not know the costs of our praise!"

I knew one in particular could hurt me very badly as he had done to others in the past but I did not care and was prepared to put them in his place at all cost. They stood there shocked at my response, and attempted to acknowledge to me "I knew you both were suffering . . ." I really did not care to hear anything coming from their mouths and walked away.

At this point in my life already been humiliated by so many leaders I could not fear anymore their threats of possible violence or whatever.

I was ready to stand for my faith in what I knew our Heavenly Father did for me and my son.

It may be difficult to understand the hatred individuals in your circles have toward people who are hurting. They see the abused as "senseless" little children who should run back home to daddy. David said in his ***Psalm 27:10,*** *"When my mother and father forsake me, He (Our Creator) will take me up?"* This is a true saying. Which part of that verse these leaders not understand? Or do they think they have the authority to nullify His words and replace them with their statistics. Our Creator says what He means and means what He says. He will not abandon you. He will provide good leaders; counselors, teachers, and friends, other family substitutes, His Holy Spirit will teach you rightly, be a father for you and your children, and help keep you in perfect peace. He means it.

Whenever a leader, stranger, family member, or friend decide to take an oppressive stand against you in speech, false accusations, misperceptions, inappropriate conduct, abuse of authority and trust against you, they have already prepared to position themselves to exercise false authority and power to rule over you with deep oppression.

I am constantly thankful for all good and true individuals including leaders in the world who are doing their best promoting healing in their communities and are not swayed by evil leaders in their communities.

What the Heavenly Father wants me to learn here is this:

When all authorities in this world: home, political, religious, and other kinds of authorities recognizes the full authority of our Creator over all people and in all things in this world, home, in religious communities, and in the work He has given them, then they will recognize their full responsibilities, accountabilities, and their limitations of power He has given them.

No one on this earth deserves such honor and respect, more than what is necessarily due to them to get along harmoniously. Limit your interactions with these abusive people and their access in your life.

True leaders recognize their own limitations, accountabilities, and responsibilities to others, have a close relationship with Him in developing right character needed to be counselors to anyone. They do not see themselves only as authorities, but helpers/counselors to others on all levels. They care about you and not behave repulsively toward you because of what you are experiencing.

False leaders/bad individuals are the opposite. They are not connected to the Father's principles: commandments, laws, statutes, and judgments even if they know and practice it outwardly. They nurture jealousies, insecurities, and hatred in their hearts. They create misperceptions against you in their circles.

Many take advantage of young, weak, wicked, insecure, and immature people who adore them, train them to walk among us as stool pigeons, servants of darkness, not as light bearers nurturing the darkness in them. They too perceive you as not belonging to their circle and they are correct; but do not perceive the darkness within themselves and hate the light of the Father in you.

His presence in you is asking them what is wrong with them, and they hate that presence not knowing.

Many faithful and wise religious leaders who are doing their best to correct them are often hated by these people who are strong in their hatred for good.

Many wicked individuals are repulsed by your singleness and your zeal for increased knowledge to improve yourself and intimacy with the Heavenly Father. They may perceive you an imagined threat to their level of knowledge, status, or position of authority, and will use evil individuals in the work place, community, or place of worship with the intent to hurt you, and to eliminate you. Some will pretend they are repulsed by such evil acts when exposed but deep in their soul they are satisfied of the results and secretly congratulate these evil acts.

I had experienced many more very painful incidents when leaders viciously demanded I return to the abuser, even at the point where I almost lost my life as a result of my over enlarged heart, and of their vicious threats to physically assault me. They had no concern for our well-being and treated me as a stubborn and rebellious little girl who should be ordered back home to daddy.

Wicked individuals attempting to usurp their false authority and power were in actual fact telling me that I was not worth real love, nor any dignity, and if it was up to them the Father would reject me too. They have even refused to talk and pray with me.

In their hostility toward you they are declaring that the abuser has the right to continue abuse on you because they perceive the abuser is the rightful authority over you and you are only property for the abuser. They want you to be fearful of them and lose yourself.

Yet our Heavenly Father says in ***Romans 8:15,*** *"For you did not receive the spirit of bondage again to fear, but you received the spirit of adoption by whom we cry, Abba, Father."*

Where is their rightful authority in wanting you to stay in bondage when our Creator says, "NO!"? And who is your rightful daddy, certainly not these abusive authorities nor the abuser.

In ***Exodus 20:2,*** the very beginning of the Commandments, when He was reintroducing Himself to a very discouraged, hurt, and angry people of whom He was to them: *"I am the Lord your God who brought you out of Egypt, out of the land of bondage. You shall have no other God to set against me."*

He was very compassionate reintroducing Himself to a very tired and desperate people—you, the victim of abuse. You have been through much sorrow and you need to know you belong with Him. He was, still is, and will ever be your only leader, the abusers had no claims on you, and you had no identity with them.

The Father had cleansed you of the evil and filthy garment attached onto your soul through abuse. You are walking free and growing in Him and educating yourself to be of success. Often evil individuals look for people they assume are malleable to target and to transfer their evil and degenerate filthy past onto you, then attempt to turn you into what they were and still are—unclean. Their excuse is: If I can do this to you then something is wrong with you or it has to do with something in your past life. They may also have said this because you have not taken a strong stand against them from the onset of their behavior.

Psalm 103:12*—"As far as the east is from the west, so far has he removed our transgressions from us.*

When you ask the Heavenly Father to forgive you of your past sins, He does that; put them far away from you and Him. Your past life has nothing to do with their misconduct. These individuals are still experiencing great difficulties in been cleansed of their evil garments of sin—their great baggage and burdens of the past, they have not repented of, and want to transfer them unto you. They say this to relieve themselves of all responsibilities and accountabilities to you, themselves, their community, and to our Creator and can be held liable for their actions of violence toward you and their communities. Stand firm against this and ask the Father to cleanse you of the evil and dark garments they are throwing at your soul to destroy you.

If a strong love and respect for such leaders had been your main focus in searching for and knowing the Heavenly Father, the enemy will use this against you as a tool of discouragement and offense in the attempt to destroy you.

When you have made the Heavenly Father your full authority and Shepherd in your life, you will not want to stay nor return to an abuser and the abusive environment, nor ever be subjected to an abusive leader. Not for all the gold and silver in this world can cause you to exchange all this growing process to revert back to be abused and kept down. Even when it might be tempting to be joined to another intimate relationship without the Shepherd's permission, His rod and staff will be there to redirect your focus. His rod and staff are His words of instructions and hope, His presence to keep you focused. You must allow the healing process He is walking you through to be completed and perfected.

Chapter twenty

YOU WILL HEAL

After leaving the abusive home you will experience healing and may experience physical pains in the process. The physical pains sometimes are interpreted as withdrawal symptoms of what the body had become accustomed to enduring, as in the case of nicotine or drug abuse withdrawal symptoms. However, that is far from this case of abuse, they are the actual pains through the many forms of abuses inflicted on the body, mind, and soul was forced to endure and to contain.

While in the hospital emergency department after leaving, I tried to explain to the doctor what I was experiencing. I could not explain it, the words could not come, but he understood what I was experiencing and trying to say.

His advice was: "This is the first step in your healing. During those years of abuse you kept it all in—distress, pain, anxieties and fears, the body and soul was forced to hold unto, now that you made the decision to leave, the body will start to release all that. Many symptoms will surface and you may think you will die. You won't, welcome it all and deal with them one symptom at a time. It will be extremely painful but you will heal. Your doctor will help you. If you need to come back here come without feeling bad. Get your family doctor to refer you to a counselor. I will send to your family doctor the immediate treatment to begin your healing. Here is my card if you need to see me in my office call and see me. We are here to help you."

While in his attempt to comfort me he showed me the x-ray of my over-enlarged heart and the result of the blood work revealing an extremely high level of non-biological toxins. I immediately contact my son's school and instructed them to have him tested as well. The result was the same but on a very low level. He also needed immediate treatment.

Our current family physician had done specific tests to determine treatment, but after confirming we were poisoned, he totally abandoned us and we could not refer ourselves for this specific treatment. He had refused to treat us. I felt we were actually left to die and I experienced great despair. It was a time of total darkness for us before we finally got treatment.

The emergency physician was extremely correct. We began to recognize what each symptom represents and how they were affecting us. They were extremely painful and felt many times we would die, but the symptoms had to be dealt with individually and sometimes together.

I spoke to people about this and was helped to contact another doctor who tried without success to obtain our treatment from the Medical Toxicologist. They were given the medical results but openly refused to treat us. He then without wasting time referred us to another specialist—naturopathic specialist and they worked together to save our lives. During our treatment he continued to monitor our health. I am ever thankful to this doctor, who died shortly after. He had worked very hard setting us on the right path of healing

Then after a team of doctors including haematologist, chiropractor, internists were working together to save our lives and help us heal. It took a great deal of effort on our part to physically in our weakened condition attend treatments, but as a result we saw the love of our Creator expressed through these doctors working together to save our lives and continue to monitor our healing.

After the first year of our successful treatment we were contacted by the Medical Toxicologist for treatment. At this point in our already successful treatment, it became a question of trust for us after their numerous rejections to even care to meet with us to determine our treatment. If we had not begun treatment during those times we certainly would have died. They only responded because our new family lawyer had read the report and contacted them demanding their accountability and responsibility to treat us.

People have their opinions about who we are, why we dare to step out on our own to survive. Will we be a burden to them? Who cares what they think. They are not the sustainer of our lives. Our Heavenly Father sent new friends, the right counselors and physicians in our lives to help keep us stable.

During our time of healing, we both received counselors who did their best to help keep us stable, help us set goals, research them, pursue them, and reset our lifestyle. As a result we were able to recognize and understand many of the cruelties we endured over the years while the processes of healing continued.

Only when you are free and allow yourself the freedom to be healed in every way the anxieties will be allayed; as a result your passion for life and true growth will resurface. You will learn the truth of what was happening to you and why, and how close you may have come in losing your life without a chance for knowing who your true Creator is and be truly connected to him.

The Israelites in Egypt were to return to their own land where they were exiled from to reclaim their property given to them as an inheritance. Before their exile in Egypt, our Creator told Abraham that they will return to their land of inheritance, and why.

Genesis 15:16—*"But the fourth generation shall return here, for the Amorites will not be ripe for punishment until then."*

This is indeed a strange paradox; the Israelites returning to the same place, where they previously were mistreated. Yet, only to witness the fall of that nation who abused them, and had caused them to flee to another place to be mistreated again in worst ways, but not without witnessing their punishment.

They were not instructed to return to the abusers for more distress. What He is saying here:

(1) They will before and after leaving the present abuser—Egypt, witness Egypt's destruction.
(2) They will witness the destruction of the Amorites who greatly oppressed them causing them to leave their own countries.

And in returning to their own land they received correct instructions for healing and success to implement for each generation in their own land.

On their way some obeyed and were healed, many did not, and regardless of massive attempts in encouraging them to remain focus and heal they chose to cherish painful memories of the past out there in the wilderness—living out each new, horrific, terrible, and unnecessary painful situations.

The main focus of His fierce determination was keeping His promises to Abraham and Moses in protecting the future of the young who left Egypt and of those born in freedom. If the adults were given the chance to return to Egypt, the young ones whom He nurtured their future would be cut off suddenly and be subjected to worse abuse.

Worst abuse, because the young ones who left Egypt with their parents had already experienced and witnessed the pain and trauma of slavery, intense abuses, and chronic distresses. They would be extremely hurt as a result of their parents' deliberately subjecting them to that all over again—indicating to them: that living in abuse would be easier than freedom because they would not need to exert such energy to be free. To be separated from their Heavenly Father and the good leaders who powerfully, tenderly loved and nurtured them would be death itself. It would be worse than not ever leaving Egypt.

Had they remained in Egypt they would never experience such exhilarating and immense freedom, healing, and exponential growth. And now to have it all come to an abrupt end because of parents' unwillingness to grow as a result of cherished hurt and pain of the past, and the frustration of not yet finding that permanent place of refuge.

How excruciatingly painful it would be for those born in freedom to experience that. They were willing to put their own newborns in chains and shackles and sure death sentence instead of staying free, indicating to them—"It is now your turn to suffer." His fierce determination, immense love, amazing grace, and great compassion for the slaves, and especially the young should not be subjected to this abuse anymore made it impossible for them to find their way back to the abuser—Egypt.

He caused the older generation to live and die out there in the wilderness in their rebellious stagnant growth, to nurture the young by His faithful servants and lead them to their prosperity.

Once you are free it is psychologically and spiritually impossible and in other ways for us and our children to return to that. It will take us fighting with all our being and rejecting everything we have learned and achieved to do an about-face back to the abuser, or an about-turn toward another abuser.

In *Hebrews chapter 4*, Paul used the Israelites' experiences as examples of certain results in staying angry after leaving an abusive life. After leaving they stayed angry and were not healed, but were always looking back to the abuser—Egypt. When you leave the abuser and you stay in that angry state of mind, you will not heal or grow and will easily be attached to another similar situation, or worse than what you left. Do not retard the progress of the young ones. Give them all the space and nurturing they need to grow. Many adult victims of abuse become bitter toward their children. They will witness the renewed passion for life in them and want to subject them to abuse again.

Many victims of abuse who return to the abuser or be attached to another may have rationalized that they are now stronger, smarter to endure the abuser's ill dispositions, hoping the abuse will end. No one is strong or smart enough for that kind of life.

When you entered the life of marriage/intimate relationship, you had dreams, goals, and expectations that needed to be realized but were quashed, stunted, and discouraged for a while. You left an abusive home because your survival was greatly threatened and held in a type of stasis, stuck in fearful situations.

Leaving is to bring you to a place of new beginning, new opportunities and experiences of true healing. While in the abusive home striving for safety in knowledge due to fear will not work, that safety never existed. You need to be taken out placed in the sunshine of freedom where you can find safety to grow, prosper without all the unnecessary anxieties and drama. These anxieties and drama are not healthy, very crippling, and incompatible with the need for growth, especially in chronic distresses.

REASSURANCE

Is it difficult to imagine you will heal? Try again. Our Creator will help you to see. He showed us. I will share with you a very profound dream I had before we left the abuser and the heaven he made for himself.

I was in this huge house. There were different groups of people praying having wonderful fellowship together. I desperately wanted to join one of the groups. I was however stuck in the kitchen cleaning up huge piles of dishes while this abuser was watching the television and demanding I get things for him. Suddenly a man walked through the door without opening it. He was about my height. His face was like shiny bronze his hair, clothes, and beard were sateen white, very shiny. He came up to me and asked me in a commanding yet sympathetic voice—"What is wrong?" At first I was cautious about whom he was and if I should trust Him. He looked at me with a very serious and compassionate face and repeated his question, and I decided to trust Him. At that moment I poured my heart out to hm. I told Him every burden that was on my heart. I explained to him how this man is hurting me and my son. He became grieved. He turned toward the abuser who at the same time had come up beside me suspicious about this man I was talking to. The man told him, "Look, man, I am no longer with you." Instantly the abuser was in the wall. He became affixed in the wall molded with the wood panels and was not able to move. Suddenly as I stood there the scene around me began to change dramatically and very quickly. As the scene was changing, I was afraid yet I felt I should not be afraid. The house was no longer there. I was now outside in the wide open. Other people were there, small groups of families, and I could not identify any. Apparently we were all parents with children. I saw some young people walking up a mountain. When they began to walk, at first they appeared weak and distressed, but as they walked up the mountain they became taller, beautiful, walking upright with confidence. I told my son to join them. He immediately ran to join them. As he ran he too became taller, beautiful, as he caught up to them, also walking with equal confidence. As he became taller he was wearing a service uniform I did not recognize. They were approaching the peak of the mountain at its highest point, and needed to reach the other mountain. I asked one of the parents, "How will they reach the other side, there is a huge gulf there?" She said, "Watch and see, it is the cord of faith that will take them over." I watched with apprehension as these youths reached the gulf and continued to walk across as though the gulf never existed. Immediately the gulf was closed and both sides of the mountain joined together and became one. I was very elated. I realized that these parents allowed their children to walk the walk by faith as they continuously nurtured them with prayer and love.

The dream ended and I was reassured that we will be okay when we leave. Our Heavenly Father will make good things happen for us, and because we put our trust in Him we will overcome the trials of life. He showed me clearly that the abuser no longer will be in our life in any way. He came into the enemy's territory to take us out completely.

After leaving an abusive home, do not follow the popular statistics about the future of children who were victims of abuse, to determine their future. We must say to and tell our children how to live healthy lives, reset lifestyles, to live in faith to be successful in life. They will experience difficulties but these will only be springboards of successes in a closer relationship with their Creator. This dream became affixed in my mind permanently, and a source of great comfort through many rough times.

You were not given freedom to be stuck in wilderness experiences-constant crippling reruns/reoccurrences of crisis you not willing to let go. His purpose is to take you out, become part of your life, help you identify your potentials and help provide opportunities to develop them into abilities to help others. In freedom, problems/crisis may come but you will learn to avoid those repetitions and deal with them effectively.

Contrary to popular beliefs indicating victims of abuse do not heal is contrary to what this dream revealed and what He said in *Isaiah 61*, speaks of the suffering servant, YaHoshua—the Messiah. If he had not died for us we would not have freedom from abuse.

In *Isaiah 61*, *He came to "bring good news to the humble, and to bind up the broken hearted."* That is you; constantly crying out to Him for deliverance and healing of a broken heart because of abuse. He heard your cry and will help you. He came to *"proclaim liberty to captives and release to those in prison."* That you were too and your children, held captive by the abuser and his demons for so long. An abusive home is a prison *"institution"* the abuser created as a haven to hold you captive unto them. Clearly what you were enduring was not good for you, and you were to experience good in your life, and know that one day he will take revenge on the enemies. He came to *"comfort all who mourn, to give beauty for ashes, oil of gladness instead of mourning, and a garment of praise instead of a spirit of despair."* He came to comfort you and make you beautiful again and more beautiful than before. Abuse gives garments of violence and heaviness that covered you, they are to be removed and replaced with a vibrant spirit, beauty, joy, and praise in your heart toward Him.

Wicked individuals who wanted to shovel you back to the abusers what they meant; "You had sexual intimacy with your abuser and only the abuser to have that relationship with you for the rest of your natural life regardless how perilous your situation was, and if you have another partner you are committing adultery."

They are saying you are not deserving of real love or true freedom. They are claiming you must stay with that partner simply because you had sex with that partner, they are repulsed by your situation, and some will look on at you as unclean and want you out of their sight because of the violence you suffered. Some will see your singleness as vulnerability and an opportunity to violate you. Some had tried that with me and I got help to reprimand them. To this day I am not liked for that, but I really, really, do not care.

Perish and expunge those thoughts in your mind of such lingering futile and destructive connections to an abuser.

Hebrew 4:12—"*For the word of God is alive and active. It cuts more keenly than any two-edged sword, piercing as far as the place where life and spirit; joints and marrow divide, It sifts the purposes and thoughts of the heart, there is nothing in creation that can hide from him; everything lies naked and exposed to the eyes of the One with whom we have to reckon.*"

The Heavenly Father took the multitude of slaves out of Egypt, totally severed the bonds they had with Egypt—sexually, emotionally, financially, mentally, physically, spiritually, and politically. Then He gave them instructions in staying free and connecting permanently with Him. Many obeyed and were healed in every way. Many chose not to and died as a result without the hope of eternal life.

Living in an abusive environment only causes you and your children to live at cross purpose with our Creator's plans for your lives. Their lives will become derailed, their efforts frustrated, and they will begin to die as a result of pain and frustration that this unhealthy environment gives.

We do not know how tangled our emotions and souls are with traumatic results of abuse and the painful connections to abusers. The pain is real and cannot be sorted out in one day or on our own. We would not know where to start. This divine operation and healing our Creator knows the beginning and ending of such entanglements and how to sever those connections with no damage done to you, patiently take you through the processes of healing, and shield you from abusers. Allow these processes and you will not have the desire for that or any other abuser.

Monitor very closely your children's emotional and spiritual connections to the abuser to determine if they are carrying any unnecessary burdens and to determine if they may want to continue the abuser's evil behavior.

After leaving the abuser, we were able to obtain professional and caring counselors who worked hard with us to help keep us stable, set goals, research them and accomplish them in timely manner. As a result were able to understand many of the cruelties we experienced over the years.

You are teaching your children about themselves in what our Creator said *in Exodus 20, "I am the Lord your God who has taken you out of Egypt out of the land of bondage."* What He is also saying here: *I am your sovereign Lord, who delivered you from your pain and suffering. You were mine and still mine. I have totally severed the connections between you and the abuser. Do not look back in any way toward them, nor toward another. They had the chance to treat you right and did not. I am here to heal you in every way if you allow me.*

Another proof of healing—***Psalm 23:3a*** *"He restoreth my soul."*

Webster's Dictionary defines:

Restore *v.t. build up again, repair renew; re-establish; give back.*

Our Heavenly Father wants to continue repairing all the damages done to you and your children. He will continue sorting them out and heal you step by step while building you up again. As you continue to research and work on all your goals you will begin to understand what you endured, and repair the breaches in your life; damaged family and friendship relationships, work, health, and restoring of goals. Work to re-establish His principles, love, and beauty in you and give you a heart of praise, and good things that were missing in the marriage.

Fill your mind with His instructions. Fear will gradually be replaced with joy. You can look back at different stages of your life and ask Him "You did this for me?" You will begin to see you and the children's purposes for life, and encourage them to hold onto that cord of faith to make it through each day, take that giant leap of faith and do what is right to succeed. You will be amazed at how much He is willing to do for them.

He will keep His angels charge to protect you, comfort you, talk with you, instruct, and show you where you are in your circumstances, and how to avoid unnecessary terrible future pains.

Do not allow your past experiences to keep you in fear. Step out those areas of fear into the wide unknown where you will not stop learning. Trust Him to do for our children what we cannot do for them, and tell them of this decision. I often remind my son, "Never forget what He has taken us out of. Imagine what His plans are for you." Teach them it is better to fail trying than not to try at all. They may not succeed at everything but in their attempt they will experience growth, knowledge, understanding, wisdom, and discernment to live good quality life.

He was encouraged to continue with his extracurricular activities. He did and is successful in those areas most beneficial to him for his future to help mankind, a very powerful healing process for him. He needs to know that—not because we left an abuser means our life is on hold and he is to park his talents and skills that were very important to him. He must learn to pick up from where he left off and walk in faith. At times he was ill and needed time from school to avoid a relapse.

He did not become emotionally or intellectually dead as those wicked people falsely prophesied against him.

Our levels of intelligence and abilities to develop our skills to prosper did not originate with an abuser. They originated with the Creator in His design for us long before we were created and before the abuser came in existence and in our lives.

He was taken out for a reason—complete healing and prosperity. The Creator saw the plans He had for my son would not succeed in that dark environment. He must be taken out put in another environment where there is light and space to be healed and restored for success to happen in his life.

Chapter twenty-one

EMOTIONAL HEALING—CALL TO HIS GRACE

One of the most important elements of your suffering is the gift of our Creator's amazing grace: His Holy Spirit communicating with us. It serves the purpose of allowing you to see yourself, your children, and your lack of progress in your stagnant position. As painful as that sounds, you may not have known you were in extreme pain without the nerves in your body communicating to you via pain. This grace communicates to us in profound ways and warns us of danger, lack of growth, and that something needs to be done or you will die. Each day, be very thankful you are alive and come to this realization you need help.

In the abusive home correct principles for living were blocked from your life, misinterpreted, and incorrectly lived out as an example to you. You felt you were in danger because the abuser wanted to control you instead of controlling his/her own fears.

You became profoundly aware of your state of danger that threatens your future. Welcome it, be thankful to the Creator always for life, and do not stay in your state of doubt. Question it and research those answers for possible solutions.

Everyone in this world is called to the existence of His grace and to the restoration of His principles in them, but only few accept grace due to fear, anxieties, lack of knowledge, procrastination, etc. This grace requires you taking that giant leap of faith to grow. You may suddenly come to the realization that you are in a bad position, a dangerous state, and you may die. How that came about was by His call to grace working through people or through you. It is not a state of paranoia, it is real.

http://www.biblegateway.com/resources/commentaries/IVP-NT/Matt/Scorning-Kings-Son

If you really want emotional healing for yourself, your children and all those you have impacted accepting grace you will need to welcome His grace. The welcoming of both good and bad *(v. 10) echoes Jesus' own mission to sinners (9:11-13), but it may also remind us that grace not only forgives but also transforms. All are welcome, but no one dare remain the way he or she entered.*

The deep desire to escape an abusive environment, recognizing you and your children are in a state of danger will require a determined will to step out into the unknown knowing you will experience good. Your refusal to this call to grace is form of suicide a slow death to self in every way as a result of allowing yourself to continuously bleed—emotionally and physically as you continue to nurture doubts and fears, eventually die, a literal death which requires your family members and friends to bury you in a cemetery plot.

When we step out in faith we are saying, "My children and I are finally ready to heal with all the challenges that will come, we are not alone," and you will begin to see the emotional needs of your children. They need to reconnect with family and friends who were barred from your lives while in the abusive home.

Often times you may feel alone as though the whole world has rejected you. It is not so. The abusers are not the whole world, neither is the universe centered on them nor about them. It is about new and better beginnings. Ask our Heavenly Father to extend your territories of family and friends and He will. Some friends we had to leave behind for good reasons. We met and establish some good friendships that last to this day and have become extensions of family for us. Constantly avoiding people by keeping to yourselves will only foster an environment of isolation and vulnerability for you and your children. In a state of loneliness despair sets in very easily as memories of past abuses used to nurture the present.

When you become discouraged find a quiet spot and pour your heart out to our Creator for guidance, help, and deliverance. There are days and nights your soul will really need to deeply connect with Him, read His words of assurances to remind you of His promises of deliverance, healing, and restoration.

You are on your own with children who will occasionally become angry. Do not be afraid. Not all friends can be trusted with problems about your children. Call on your support of friends or family members who you and your children trust. Encourage it because your children will need someone to talk with as well, who will understand deeply what they are experiencing and who was actively involved before and during this healing process. And more importantly will listen when they need to bear their soul.

Let's be fair, we as parents really need someone to talk with more so our children. Even if you call the number and hear them bear their soul while you listen or not to their conversations. It is okay and very refreshing to them that you care enough about them to listen and allow them to vent their heart's sorrows. It is one of the most powerful tools of healing you can give them. My son talks about me. Our children will talk about us whether we like it or not. They will talk to their friends, other teenagers, and adults about how they feel and they need this outlet, providing they are not encouraged against us. Let your children know you know this but must be in a respectful manner.

YOU WILL GLOW

Often times you may recognize your healing process. You begin to feel free in your soul, and may still continue to experience pain because you are still hurting and healing at the same time. You are beginning to experience peace in your life and you feel it.

Peace is a rare commodity society often declares. Everyone needs peace. Some are desperate for it and some only want it. Our Savior—YaHoshua; *"My peace I give unto you not as the world giveth, but as I giveth."—**John 14:27**.* To wake in the morning and go through your day and return to bed in peace is not easy. The first day my son came to live in our new home, we sat on the couch and breathed that peaceful air. It was an awe moment for us. I told him, "Listen to that sound, so peaceful. No sound of abuse around." He felt so relieved for it. We sat on the couch for a very long time in silence and enjoyed it, and I saw his relief as the spirit of oppression left him.

A man once gave his testimony. He spoke of the struggles he experienced in life and the pain he endured. He explained that even though he endured all that and had passed through all that,

Peace is not the absence of struggle, it is the assurance that through it all, your mind is able to stay focused on our Creator.

That is very true. Faith is a living experience. If you have never experienced what I am talking about, not know of anyone who has been through an abusive situation, nor care about people who experienced this, or living in denial, it would be difficult for you to understand what I am talking about. It is to have total trust in our Creator even when you do not feel like it, regardless of what is happening in you and around you.

Do not allow the wounds of abuse to fester forever; now is the time to be healed permanently. If you have a physical festering wound that needs medical attention, the physician will tell you it needs to be opened, drained, washed with the right solution, apply medication, sutured up if necessary, and sealed up to be healed permanently. There may be scars remaining but you can apply ointment to remove the scars. That is how it is with emotional wounds and scars as deep as yours. It needs to be reopened, drained, washed, sutured, sealed up, and anointed to be healed permanently.

Opening wounds can be excruciatingly painful, not pretty or painless. If the infected part is not treated, you will either lose function of that part of your body, or it could infect the rest of your body and may kill you. By pouring out your heart each day in prayer of thankfulness, you are totally allowing your wounds to reopen. You will come to know you had more injuries than you ever thought you had and the wounds are painful. You are releasing the burdens that were not yours to carry from the beginning. Also talk to a counselor or a good friend who will give you immediate feedback. Our Creator is satisfied with you talking to Him alone about your problems, He would not mind. But He knows you need human interactions for instant feedback and who can be active in your life to help you see possible solutions to your everyday trials. With the help of caring professional counselors we were successful in our studies and healing.

BEAUTY FOR ASHES

*In **Isaiah 61:1–3***, we learned the mission of the Savior, our Messiah, who left the most beautiful and holy place to save us.

Isaiah 61:1–3, *"The Spirit of the Lord God is upon me because the Lord has anointed me; he has sent me to bring good news to the humble, to* *bind up the broken hearted, to proclaim liberty to captives and release to those in prison; to proclaim a year of the Lord's favor and a day of the vengeance of our God; to comfort all who mourn, to give them beauty instead of ashes, oil of gladness instead of mourner's tears, a garment of splendor—praise for the heavy heart. They shall be called Trees of Righteousness, planted by the Lord for his glory."*

We often sing this passage of scripture in a song but never understood its meaning until we have a profound experience, good or bad. When you are going through a crisis it shows, but only for a short period of time. When you are living in a crisis, it transforms you from the inside outward—your appearance, and your life. People can preach it but do not experience it. We try to explain it away but cannot understand its depth until we have experienced it ourselves.

When going through an abusive situation, you cannot dress well enough to look good. True beauty comes from the inside and shines outward; that no matter how casually nice and simple you dress you will look gorgeous.

Decide from now if you have not left the abusive home, what kind of life you want—choose: normal vs. healthy.

Society refers to normal life as a pattern of living, whether good or bad, to fall in their patterns and expectations of you. Sounds familiar? The abuser's idea of a normal life with you is where they could on a regular basis pour out on you hurt and pain. It was not normal for you and only proved to be very unhealthy and your health suffered as a result. However, it was normal for the abuser's regular pattern of behavior which almost killed you.

Webster's Dictionary defines:

Normal. *A. perpendicular, conforming to type, ordinary Health v.t.—restore to health, made well, cure—. V.t. become sound n.—soundness of body, condition of body, toast drunk in a person's honor a.—having, or tending to give, health, a.—health giving.*

Do you get the picture? The negative people in your circle wanted you to live a life that they consider normal to them—cope and live with abuse. They wanted you to conform to their idea of healthy life and lead you into depression and ultimately insanity and death. One person's idea of healthy may definitely not be yours, especially when you are desperate to break your way out of your four walls of abuse.

An abused person who longs to escape and have escaped is not and should not be interested in living a regular normal life. Normal was the story of your life for too long—stuck with an ordinary spouse whose behavior was killing everything healthy in you; stuck in a shelter type nothing but a prison for you; stuck listening to negative, stupid, and wicked people telling you to stay in it—for so long. However long it was, it was too long.

You are only interested in getting out of that. You have goals that will not be quenched by anyone's view of healthy life for you. You know the goals you craved are attainable regardless of your present predicament and will not accept what does not give soundness of health in all areas you desire to restore. The healthy life you crave does not exist with the abuser.

By Marianne Williamson: **http://skdesigns.com/internet/articles/quotes/williamson/our_deepest_fear/**

"Our deepest fear is not that we are inadequate. Our deepest fear is that we are powerful beyond measure. It is our light, not our darkness that most frightens us. We ask ourselves, who am I to be brilliant, gorgeous,

talented, and fabulous? Actually, who are you not to be? You are a child of God. You're playing small does not serve the world. There is nothing enlightened about shrinking so that other people won't feel insecure around you. We are all meant to shine, as children do. We were born to make manifest His glory that is within us. It's not just in some of us; it's in everyone. And as we let our own light shine, we unconsciously give other people permission to do the same. As we are liberated from our own fear, our presence automatically liberates others."

Chapter twenty-two

PROTECTING YOUR HEART

In an abusive situation, facing our Red Sea and keeping guard of our mind is hard work. I remembered in the last year before I left I prayed a lot, constantly fasting and praying for guidance. Many people would say at that point, "You are praying for the wrong reason, darling. You should instead pray for you and your husband's behavior to improve." Well, the Indian proverb says this, *"Do not judge a man until you have walked a mile in his moccasins."* Often while praying, the abuser kept interrupting my prayers insulting me saying, "You are wasting time praying, all you need to do is be obedient." That only gave me one more kick in the butt to pray more fervently for help to get out.

Knowing who the source of your strength is can save your life. The abuser knows you will succeed and wants to discourage your efforts for a better life because they know they have nothing good to offer you.

Some abusers often pretend they repent to keep their victims in their shadow. For me trusting that will take the King of Glory Himself telling me that is so.

When I was a child I saw this: when victims of abuse leave the abusers, the abusers will suddenly attend a place of worship very often in desperate attempts to show their repentance. This will continue for months, until everyone is convinced in their assumptions that the abuser has repented.

The religious leaders' trust, lack awareness and responsibilities to counsel and command proof of the abuser's repentance only entreated the victims to return.

The victims of abuse expressed their great fear of the Creator, guilt for leaving the scoundrels, and some hope in the process of returning, return to the abuser. The abusers immediately began to repeat their behavior and in worst ways.

They used the places of worship and the religious leaders as their authority and their dead conscience in commanding their victims return to them; because they know the legal authorities in society will not do that for them. Through their false acts of religious piety they were able to successfully convince the religious leaders and religious communities of their false repentance. This does not mean some abusers will not truly repent, but most do not.

While in your abusive situations, some people may try to cause you to feel guilty for wanting to leave. "The children will suffer, it's not right to leave a marriage/relationship after so many years, how will you find another spouse, how will you survive without a spouse, how the children will cope without the other parent. . .," and the list goes on.

Staying in that abusive environment due to guilt will not help you anymore than wanting to die a miserable and unfulfilled person. Staying, returning, or attaching yourself to another abuser will give the message they are right in thinking and telling you the rubbish that you cannot survive without them. They will play Russian roulette with you until you either lose your mind or die. Determine in your mind if this is what you want, stay or leave. If you decide to leave, be determined to leave in every way and not return to the abuser, nor be attached to another in the future.

You are not leaving one abuser for another. Your life is not about *stress management;* that is what living with abuse is—*stress management*—a total waste of time, always counting and balancing your losses.

You need freedom for *self-management*, where you can grow healthy and succeed. *Self-management* is about having the freedom and responsibility to manage yourself successfully; to develop your abilities to make right decisions that matters in all areas of life and to cope with situations and circumstances in healthy ways that benefits everyone, have a life of harmony, true wealth (big or small), true love, good health, and financial freedom.

You have had enough of this rubbish, and it is time for your beautiful self to come alive again, be restored, bloom, and be more beautiful than before. Your beautiful self has been buried and suppressed far too long in that abusive home. You need to bring it back and be improved. If you are not sure how get some help to achieve this. There are many resources available to accomplish this. This is your learning time; about yourself and will need to be more educated in your true identity to the Creator. You were created to identify your potentials and abilities to be a conduit of His light to help others heal and succeed.

This newfound freedom is extremely powerful, designed to establish you in His truth by first delivering you from all forms of evil displayed in your Egypt, help you to see yourself in it and your helplessness, you are not to continue with the evils of the past, and preventing you from indulging in other forms which exist in your new environment of growth.

Your new place of true growth is not dependent on the evils that exist around you but on your total dependence and obedience to the Creator, and your desire for restoration and in all areas of life.

In ***Leviticus 18:1–5, Deuteronomy 11, 12***, our Creator had instructed and encouraged the multitude of slaves who had left their Egypt to live their lives with thankfulness, courage, and purity by not indulging in any evils that existed there nor which exist in their new home of freedom. These were illustrated throughout the book of Leviticus and repeated throughout the entire Bible. They struggled with oppositions and feelings of past oppression, some stayed courageous, while some did not and suffered.

You will be met with oppositions of various kinds after leaving the abusive environment. These oppositions are fears expressed by the messenger of discouragement to block your path preventing you from experiencing true healing and growth to recognize the potentials the Creator has in place for you to identify and walk in. *Welcome to our Creator's battlefield.*

Insecure married and single people will be a source of test for you. You may suddenly realize you are in another world, a world of singlehood and you are viewed not as a single person who never married but as a married person who may be looking for another mate. Depending on your community of affiliation you may be viewed as a threat to others. While with your spouse no one ever saw you as a threat, why now you are a threat? You will now see other evils which were hidden from your eyes are now shown and displayed to you. Then you will begin to understand the Heart of our Heavenly Father how He feels about their behavior.

Marriage is not a requirement to have a relationship with our Creator or for eternal life; but an intimate relationship between man and woman requires this commitment in a relationship with Him. If having an intimate partner to see our Creator was a requirement, I know I will miss out and so would many other married couples who are not living right.

Many married individuals are very insecure and are not comfortable with someone in your position. Some may try to engage you into unwholesome marriage discussions, to cause you to feel you are not normal and something is wrong with you living good quality life without an intimate partner. Married women had tried to put me in a bad position to discuss with them why I left the abuser, by speaking of individuals who had left their spouse for simple misunderstanding and then proceeded in the attempt to interrogate me to explain my reason for leaving. I refused to be drawn into that type of discussion with anyone.

Be confident and let them know that your life and you leaving the abuser is not about them. It is about you been in the position where the Creator wants you to be restored in every way to be the beautiful, healthy, educated, and successful person He intended you to be.

When you leave this abusive home, seek help to understand what your weaknesses were and what caused you to be involved with this person; what were the obvious and subtle signs of the abusive behavior you ignored; what strengths you thought you had to cope with such causative dispositions. Take your time to meditate and research on these before considering another intimate relationship. The answers may not come all at once; and for your mind's stability it will not because you may not be able to endure it. Wisdom and understanding take time to be acquired; the kind that can only come through grace. He will give you power of discernment to spare you from future pains and losses, yourself, and other abusers. This newfound freedom is to help you in your healing and restoration. Try to accomplish all the good that you could not while in the abusive home.

Allow yourself the opportunity to be in a place of being—wholeness and oneness; to learn who you were created to be in His plans for you; to be a healthy, happy, and unique individual.

Resolve in your soul to allow no one the opportunity to push you into relationships you are not ready for. Be determined to be happy with yourself first before getting involved again. You will be a better and more mature person.

Many things are new after leaving such an awful estate. Victims of abuse are often vulnerable because they are in the mode of trusting, comfort, and wanting to be friendly and desiring for someone to respect and maybe to love. Yet, we must realize that we are still healing and He is not done yet. He is zealously and jealously guarding our souls. He knew what we experienced and what the end results are as He intended for us. Allow no one to interfere with that progress. This does not mean you will never find a loving person. There are many good decent and loving persons out there who can make healthy contributions to your already fulfilled life.

Refuse to begin new relationships with persons of questionable character traits thinking you are strong enough to work it out all by yourself and no one to interfere. Bad idea! Abuse and abusers come in many forms and behave very differently.

Never ignore the character traits of an abuser when shown to you, whether others see or perceive them, thinking you now have the strength to counteract them. People who love us and are truly caring can see what we cannot see, things we may have a hint of but too close to see the big picture. Before entering another relationship pray and take the time to seek guidance/counsels from wise individuals. If they are not good for you Our Heavenly Father will sieve these characters for you, and allow them to play out before your eyes.

Constantly take the time for self-analysis and review of your growth processes to determine what you have learned and still need to learn.

This is not a rush project, you really need to deliberately take the time to do this frequently and carefully.

Often people would ask me if I am in contact with the abuser, if he repent would I return. It is not my responsibility to think of the abuser's well-being. These are very distressful questions with intent to stir up old wounds and to keep me in a victim mindset. Most who asked these questions are not concerned about the abuser proving to them repentance; they just want to shuffle me back to him, out of their sight and to my grave. I firmly told them I am not interested, not open for discussion, and leave me alone. Some do not mean any harm and will understand.

While in a group of women, we were approached by other women who had escaped their vicious abusers were excited with the prospect of another marriage had the audacity to assume the role of marriage counselors to us; "Ladies you all need a man in your life. Why not return to your abusive husbands, maybe he repent you never know?" We immediately reprimanded them: "Why don't you go back to your vicious and psychotic abusive ex-husbands, they may have repented, you never know? Why, you see us single happy women as threats to your future marriage? If that's the attitude you have against us, you are definitely not ready for marriage." Of course they got remarried and it never worked out.

The option for turning back does not exist for me. It is about my freedom. I can sing songs of freedom." This freedom is too exhilarating for me to ever turn back. I felt so light and free as thousands of pounds of distresses are off my back. There is no way I would give up that freedom in exchange for any abuser. There is not enough money in this world to lure me back to that or to another kind.

Sexual immorality will be a test to you. This new freedom is not a new life to be sexually immoral. As the Apostle Paul admonished us in ***1 Corinthians 6:9–20***—Sexual immorality are other forms of abuse inflicted on the body, mind, and soul; designed to destroy you by blocking your pathways to be reeducated in your true identity to the Creator; prevents your healing and wholeness; prevents happiness as a single person; causes you to live in another darker and more destructive shadow preventing you from been a conduit of His light for others to be healthy; blocks all healthy forms of creativity to learn true love and to prosper; and prevents you from identifying your true potentials and abilities and success.

Sometimes people may want to question your new growth in this area. Be determined to allow no one the opportunity to lure you into any desire to be sexually immoral, or be involved in any forms of immorality. There is not enough money or wealth in the world can lure you into this, nor buy your freedom back from our Savior in exchange for a life of sexual immorality, especially when you allow Him to be in total control of your life.

The abusive environment was an immoral place to be which causes you to feel disconnected from the only true source of your being. In this place you were not taught the correct principles of life, nor were they exhibited correctly for you. Sexual immorality and all other forms of immorality are defiance to our Creator who delivered you to have the freedom to know Him, yourself, and what you can become. The abusers behaved immorally due to their disconnection from Him.

There are so many books written in the hopes of teaching single people about sex, passionate lovemaking in marriage, etc., etc., as though marriage is the only way to be happy. None of these books illustrates the correct principles of our Creator in guiding singles to be grounded, successful, and to be happy single individuals free from the vices and the devastating consequences of sexual immorality. How can these books help anyone?

Singles need to be taught on higher levels correct principles of life; principles of good living which will guide our mind and heart to true success in real love, recognizing potentials and develop our abilities to establish real career goals, avoiding unclean people and places, establishing clean and happy relationships, true wealth (big or small), and successes in family and business relationships, etc.

Insecurities of other singles in your communities:

An old man once said: "*A single person, one who is living out correct principles is never safe from the evil hearts of insecure persons, single or married.*" That is very true. Often single persons whose lifestyle was one of sexual immorality chasing after other's partners will try and accuse you of the same thing knowing they are wrong. The enemy that influenced them to do those wrongs is using them to transfer the same evil spirit unto you through false accusations because it cannot influence you to do wrong. Its purpose also is to throw their filthy garments of sin onto your soul, to cause you to feel dirty, unloved, and to stop trusting our Creator. It is looking for dry places to grow in. Get help to stand up against it. Fill your being with correct principles, praise and thanksgiving to our Creator and it will not win over you.

A lady once said to me: "*Every sin that exist in this world you will be tested by them, the reason to fortify your minds with all the instructions from our Heavenly Father. Allow no one to cause you to sin. You become tempted when you chose to entertain those sins. Quash them when you are tested. Stand in our Creator's Principles against every sin and at the end still stand against those sins.*"

Another frustration you may experience, some single people trying to cause other single individuals to feel inadequate without an intimate partner. "Everyone is doing it, what's taking you so long," and how important to have an intimate partner in my life for that purpose. I boldly inform them, "My single life of freedom is not for that purpose and my life is not open for discussion." They do not care to understand why I am not pining for an intimate partner, and my passionate desire to grow and to contribute in healthy ways to mankind. Happiness is not limited to marriage, or sexual relationships, but a life that is pleasing to our Creator.

Neither would it be healthy for your children to see you having different intimate partners in your life while still healing. They are still very young and vulnerable and need your help to heal. Your new home environment can become unsafe as they are exposed to your different partners. The right values you are attempting to restore and teach them will become obscured and the healthy development of their neurological pathways will be disturbed. They will become confused and will rebel against you. They are expecting their new home environment to be only for you and them while they are still very young. While going through the healing processes they are not ready to share such private space with another partner for fear of their abusive past revisiting them possibly in worst ways.

You need to help guard their innocence. When you the parents decide to ignore correct values you start to live a distorted life and you become an enemy to their full potentials and abilities. You cause the protective boundaries of our Heavenly Father put in place for you and your children's life to be breached and destruction follows.

Living a distorted life also distorts the values in others—friends, neighbors, family, and coworkers. You may not be aware of this; other single and married individuals who may or may not have experienced abuse are looking to you to be an example of strength. They too have struggles you may not be aware of and by observing your life of purity in the midst of your struggles, they will learn to be strong in many important areas of their lives, and as a result help others to do the same.

Years ago my friend Maggie exclaimed, "You are the reason I am not involved with guys the way I used to. I watch your life all the time." I was very shocked and it took me a long time to understand that statement and the impact I had made in her life, unaware. I was convinced she was a powerful influence in my life.

Many tried to ask me if I was ready to be sexually involved again without determining my growth process or any discussion of finding me a marriage partner. I totally refused to answer them on that, but chose instead to direct my answer to the long list and processes of growth the Creator is taking me through. They quickly get the message.

People often do not understand the deep scar abuse can cause and the bitter taste left in your mouth for such a relationship. The old saying is true: *"The heart knows its own sorrows, and no one intermeddles with its joy,"* ***Proverbs 14:10.***

BibleCommenter.com. ***The heart knoweth his own bitterness נפש מרת morrath naphsho, "The bitterness of its soul."*** *Under spiritual sorrow, the heart feels, the soul feels; all the animal nature feels and suffers. But when the peace of God is spoken to the troubled soul, the joy is indescribable; the whole man partakes of it. And a stranger to these religious feelings, to the travail of the soul, and to the witness of the Spirit, does not intermeddle with them; he does not understand them: indeed they may be even foolishness to him, because they are* *spiritually discerned.* **Biblecommenter.com. Clarke's commentary on the Bible.**

Neither can they understand your joy been in this newfound freedom, and your need for space to be healed. You will be at a place in your life where you cannot be reached. It is too private and should only be between you, our Heavenly Father, those who shared your pain, and those who can help. This peace springing up inside of me, they have no clue what that is, cannot begin to understand its true source, they heard of Him, but they cannot interrupt its flow, cannot give it, and cannot take it away. To them it is foolishness because they have not experienced it and cannot relate to it.

Ask our Heavenly Father to put His boundaries of protection around you to: preserve you as His child; educate you in His instructions while guarding and molding your character in His image; teach you how to determine boundaries with all you come in contact with; prevent abusers from coming near you, and to set you on the right path for true prosperity His way. This He did for me. He will do such a powerful and effective work in this area that you may wonder; why are they not approaching you. He did not deliver you to be attached to another abuser, nor be exploited in anyway by anyone regardless of their positions of authority reverting you back to any darkness.

When anyone attempts to cross those boundaries they are intentionally attempting to remove those boundaries to prevent your growth; setting themselves up as enemies to your potentials and abilities; to set up roadblocks in your way to have control of you and to destroy you. Stay grounded in the correct principles for your life to avoid all these and stay free. You may suffer consequences-hatred, insults, etc., but they are nothing compare to the consequences of not standing up against it. When this happens He is revealing the true dark character of the person(s) in question, and leading you to another higher level of growth in Him.

When you finally decide to have available to you the freedom to truly love yourself and all those who depend on you, you will be fiercely determined to physically and in every way take that giant leap of faith into the unknown—your Red Sea, and keep moving forward. You will learn the highest forms of love you were designed to express, are inevitably not acts of conformity.

How To Make The Leap Into The Unknown*. Posted on 03/02/2009 by mezz • 13 Comments.com http://ivancampuzano/how-to-make-the-leap-into-the-unknown/*

"There is always a way out of your trouble; and if you take the time to think clearly, to think how to get rid of the cause of your anxiety instead of just worrying about it, you become a master."—Paramhansa Yogananda

The choice to not conform to anyone's false interpretations, or false expectations of what a person should be, was a great giant leap of faith into the unknown.

Knowing that we dare to love ourselves in its purest form, is allowing ourselves to accept His grace: which will equip us for the journey of spiritual growth and requires courage, initiative, and independence of thought and action. The call of grace is what YaHoshua said: *"Many are called but few are chosen."* ***(Matthew 22:14)*** Actually implies here that all humans are called to His grace: an invitation for deliverance, healing, restoration, and growth in Him, etc. This acceptance of grace refuses all about-faces, only forward march, knowing that this journey in this newfound power you will not be alone. This is the Creator's power working in your life—*the only source of grace.*

Chapter twenty-three

WHO ARE THE FATHERLESS?

In reality there are no fatherless children—biologically. Every child was conceived by a male and female, through sexual intercourse whether by parental choice or through violence.

A *child's successes in life from birth, is not totally dependent on the birth parents—mother and father. Biological parents are: father, mother, grandparents, and all other family members and family friends. Reason for this is that in rare circumstances as listed below, children at time of their birth are separated from their families through death of the maternal/paternal parent, horrible diaspora as a result of natural disasters, famine, war, or by other acts of violence. We do not always understand nor like why these things happen but we see that children are always the final casualties.*

In ***Deuteronomy 16:14,*** our Creator calls all children without parent(s) orphans. Families were instructed to graft these orphans into families and communities to be nurtured and taught all correct principles for success. Today, children without fathers, mothers, and families need to be engrafted into families and caring communities for true nurturing, growth, healing, and maturity through correct principles for good quality living.

From the beginning of creation, our Creator had put in our DNA and our soul the ability to look at others in and outside our intimate circles to love and care for them. When we fight against it we feel a dangerous separation from Him in our soul. If we continue to resist it long enough we become cold and callous in heart. ***Genesis 3:9–11***, Cain, after killing his own brother Abel, retorted in anger when asked of his cruel actions to his brother. *"Am I my brother's keeper?"* That was a fearful statement given in response to our Creator who had put in his soul the ability to love and care for his brother Abel and others around him. As a result of his crime he immediately became permanently separated from his father Adam and from his Heavenly Father in heart and soul.

As a child growing up into adulthood, I witnessed the hurt and pain children whose father or mother have died or not present, experienced, and endured. Why should a child be judged and condemned hopeless as a result of the absence of the father—as a result of death, abandonment, divorce, relocation (father's need to travel for work), etc., be punished by society? I often wondered where this darkness come from, who started such evil thinking, should the child be blamed for the evils in their lives they have no control of? How much a child must suffer to know that they are still human and must be loved to have a bright future, even without a father? Why must the heart of these individuals become cold and callous toward these children? Are they not part of our immediate communities, society, and our future generations to replace the older ones? Are our Creator's blessings only for children with fathers who are still alive, present, and are prospering—heaven forbid if these scornful parents were to die? What would happen to their children? Would these children become recluse of society as well? Do they not consider this evil could happen to their children also?

Society, in its discrimination, does not classify who the fatherless are nor can they. Any child who falls in any of these descriptions below is called *fatherless* by society and is slated for the same fate regardless of the numerous supports in their community and family, and the child's achievements obtained as a result of hard work.

1. Children who are the casualties of war crimes, famine, natural disasters, and as a result are accidentally separated from family and or completely abandoned by parents, other family members, society, and friends, due to severe disparities as a result of these disasters. They are totally on their own. They are from all ages; babies, toddlers, and older, not old enough to develop survival skills but are forced to survive on their own. Some can be found roaming the streets day and night destitute without the help of adults or anyone to feed, nurture, and to guide them. They are without any of their own biological parents—mother and father (who may have died) or family and friends to care for them, and abandoned by prospering adults around them who have homes and see them as a threat to their own prosperity. Many people in the world rationalized why they should help. In the heart of our Heavenly Father this is extremely cruel, and his heart is soft toward these children and He considers them His own.
2. Children whose fathers are dead as a result of sickness or casualty of violence. They are also without biological fathers. Some fathers died before their children are born. However, for some, family members and the community are very constant support in their lives to love and nurture them to be healthy and successful. Some are lacking in support of others. His heart is soft toward these children also and He considers them His own.
3. Children who are victims of abuse from the biological father, adaptive, or non-adaptive parent. They are isolated with these abusers, rejected, and endangered. Due to the darkness in the hearts of the fathers, the children are separated from real love, and the love of others. Yet our Creator's heart is soft toward these children considers them His own, and above all desires their safety.
4. Children who reside with their biological fathers who treat them well and do their best to lead them the right way. All children below the age of accountability are to be taught the correct

principles and at least one commandment given to them to obey: *"Children obey your parents in the Lord for this is right. Honor your mother and father that your days may be long upon the land which the Lord thy God give thee."* (*Colossians 3:20*)

While growing up in this constant rebellion against right instructions, they disconnect themselves from the love of their biological and their Heavenly Father. Yet He desires their repentance and reconnection to their fathers.

5. Children who are conceived through violence: rape, incestuous abuse, and other forms of violence. They do not know their biological father, and it would be in their best interest to not know them or they could be subjected to the same fate or worse. Yet our Creator's heart is soft toward these children He still considers them His children, and desires their healing and safety.
6. Children, before birth, whose parents were abandoned by their expected fathers. Yet God's heart is soft toward these children He still considers them His own. In some cases, it may be in the best interest of the child to know the father, and may as a result of much counseling, reconciliation can be achieved and healing begun. God desires the hearts of the children be reunited to the fathers to grow healthy and in peace and safety, and connect with Him.
7. As adults, if our fathers had and we are not connected to our Heavenly Father, we are also fatherless. Our Creator requires our repentance and reconnection to Him.

Wicked and rebellious generations regardless of cultural and religious practice, with our without fathers, are fatherless due to separation from our Heavenly Father. The whole world needs deep cleansing from the evil we live by and only He can do it.

The enemy of our souls through the hearts of the wicked has launched an attack on children living without their biological fathers began with this rhetoric—"children without fathers are coming to nothing good." Some religious organizations in their growth of increased darkness chose to adopt this idea and carry it even further to preach it from the podium as gospel, and had woven it neatly in their bible studies and sermons. It is their duty to correct and rebuke such evil attacks on the mind of our children and society, yet blatantly refuse because to help would be in conflict with *their* own prosperity and rank wickedness.

Many good religious leaders with painful efforts to correct them are derided and mistreated by these wicked leaders. I watched many discussions with leaders on this topic, and I was appalled of the cruelties in the hearts of some leaders on the topic and their coldness toward the good leaders who have hearts of compassion and love for children and working tirelessly in caring for them.

This evil statement from wicked leaders spreads a "*veil of darkness*" on the hearts of those who are not strong and helps increase the already existing evil in the hearts of others to no longer consider exercising love for the vulnerable of society, only to hate and deride them. This becomes their gospel used as permission to nullify all affections, accountabilities, and responsibilities to our youths, including their own family members.

The youths, after hearing all this false doctrine felt the sting of hatred and rejection by leaders who claimed our Creator, their Heavenly Father loves them. They can, and most have become discouraged and hurting for a very long time. Overtime the hurt deepens. If they are not nurtured to know the truth about their future, their mind may become confused, their future derailed, and may eventually become like lost sheep with no good shepherd. Sometimes the hurt also extend into society where they will not trust any good leaders to teach them rightly. In short—at the hearing of these lies their future instantly quashed, and growth automatically become stunted.

The deep hurt is this: "If a religious leader, who is to know more than all other leaders in the world of our Creator's instructions and plans for my life say this about me, how can any leader in society tell me any different? How can I trust who is to be my Heavenly Father really care for me and have any good plans for my life? Does this mean that however hard I try to keep from evil, and follow His correct principles I will never succeed? Does this mean that no matter how I desire to know Him, obey His principles and love others, He will not hear me in my times of need?"

If this hurt continues too long and is enforced by evil family, friends, and other wicked people in society, what do we think the end will be? People need to understand that nurturing children in and out of our circles to be the best they can be will most definitely result in healthy communities for all people.

But it is the plan of the enemy and its servants—false teachers and abusers to nullify all of our Creator's Principles. In *Psalm 50:16-22*, they believe they have the authority and power to degrade all of His creation, and in a position of authority they believe He is just like them. Yet He says in verse 22—He will carve them up in pieces. They do this knowing the tragic effects they can cause, but rather see them hurt and die and reason it is conflict of interest to nurture them.

King David declared with much grief: *"When my mother and father forsake me, then the Lord will take me into His care."* (*Psalm 27:10*) David was neglected, derided, and abandoned by his own family at a delicate time of his life. He knew our Heavenly Father is his real father and will be there with him always, will put in the hearts of family, friends, neighbors to be a father and mother for you to keep you safe and stable, nurture, educate you, and keep you connected to Him.

That statement, "*Children without fathers will come to nothing good,*" is a lie straight from the pit of hell designed to: Curse our children to not believe and trust our Creator to be their Father who He has a blue print for their lives; to curse all future generations in preventing them from knowing their true identity in their true Creator and Redeemer; to question the Creator's true intent for their lives; not to believe and respect the efforts of others in society to show them the right way; not to believe they are capable of loving; and they were to die of frustration and deep depression.

Children are greatly affected by this and are vulnerable. Institutions are built to house and medicate them to be recluse of society. Society, as a result of the rejection of family and friends, and the religious organizations in our communities who do not care for these children, only see them as burdens due to the ill effects of their abandonment, now faced with the predictable results. Some of these children eventually roam the streets with no home for safety and society's hearts are cold toward them.

Children who are raised by one parent for whatever the reason of the absence of the biological fathers, who are doing their best to succeed are also looked on as immediate failures. These children with help and love of family members, friends, and rightful authorities in the communities, and with the help of our Creator became effective parents in their lives as great examples to help shield their minds from the attacks of the enemy.

Other family members are also considered *fathers/parents* for the fatherless. They are in place as family substitute; adoptive parents, legal guardians, mentors in society, family friends, and caring leaders are often times parents for many children.

My grandparents and their children were parents to many fatherless in our communities. Their hearts were gentle and kind yet firm. They cared for some of the fatherless and made sure they were educated, nurtured, loved, and have a future. Their hearts were most resolute regarding parents whose hearts were cold against their own children, and counseled them to be good to their families. Nothing and no one could convince us that dark statement can ever be true. How much a child must suffer before the heart of anyone sees the hope of our Creator for that child? The kingdom of Heaven is for *all* children.

Now as an adult I also need an earthly father and mother for guidance, this I was blessed with, not only one but a few including family members. They are mentors and family for us and they take great pride in their love for us. This is important to have a sense of belonging and nurturing against the evils of this world to help guard your soul.

As a result of this harsh reality, a new concept has been invented—"Anyone can be a father, but it takes someone special to be a dad." A very true statement as a result of the hardness of the hearts of people, but only proves that from before creation we were enabled to care for others.

The wicked people who falsely prophesied against your children's future know the correct promises and instructions are to help you, and kept it from you only to secure their own *prosperity and place in society, and only wanted their children to be prosperous*. They do not want to consider that your prosperity can help contribute to their generation's prosperities. Their statement: "Children without fathers will automatically fail in life"—cannot be found in any holy scriptures inspired by the Creator.

Did you know that our creator does not agree with their false prophecies, has already denounced it, and had a remedy for it?

Exodus 20:5-6 *"I the Lord your God, am a jealous God. I punish the children for the sins of the fathers to the third and fourth generations of those who hate me. But I keep faith with thousands, with those who love me and keep my commandments.*

Our Creator does not contradict Himself and is very clear in what He says. If your children after witnessing or leaving such a terrible estate of abuse chose to continue in the sins of the fathers, then they will be punished for the sins of the fathers, because their sins will be the same or worse than their fathers'. However, if they chose not to continue in those sins and chose to obey all His instructions to live a clean and healthy life, then He will bless them and their generations to come.

In ***Nehemiah 9,*** on returning from their diaspora to Jerusalem to rebuild the temple, the multitude of slaves were instructed to rededicate themselves, everyone, including all the fatherless/orphans. In all groups of society there is at least one fatherless child (orphan)—and they are to be cared for by someone. They were to confess all the sins of their parents: past, and present, and He will heal them. They were to recognize these sins (past and present) for what they were, confess and denounce them to overcome them whether they have participated in them or not to be healed. The same spirit of darkness that once worked in the hearts of the disobedient and evil people from the past still exist today among us.

Where are the men and women after the heart of our Creator in our societies today? Men and women of good conscience need to stand up and help lead these children through their different growth stages how to live in this world, and be good leaders in the community for others.

His pleasure is to preserve our souls from all evil. *In **Romans 12, Hebrews 3***, Paul also instructs us that now we have come to the Savior we have agreed to take unto ourselves all His principles: commandments, laws, statutes, and judgments and not continue in the sins of the fathers—we too in this present age have the same responsibility to follow the same instructions, given to denounce the sins of our parents, and have access to our Heavenly Father to receive strength to overcome. Continue to enforce these principles in your life and pronounce His blessings on them daily to help them heal in every way.

Chapter twenty-four

GUARD YOUR CHILDREN

Jeremiah 29:11

The New King James Version: *"For I know the thoughts that I think toward you, says the Lord, thoughts of peace and not of evil to give you a future and a hope."*

The New English Version Bible: *"I alone know my purpose for you, says the Lord: Prosperity and not misfortune, and a long line of children after you."*

The King James Version: *"For I know the thoughts that I have toward you, says the Lord, thoughts of peace and not of evil, thoughts to prosper you and bring you to an expected end."*

This verse in its content and true intent, given in different translation: What does it mean?

- *A future and a hope*
- *A long line of children after you*
- *To bring you to an expected end*

Does any of this sound familiar to you? As parents these are our true desire. Can anyone cancel any of these promises, or make better ones? No one can. They are life for our children.

Where do wicked people's false prophecies fit in His plans for them? Nowhere, only if you allow it. They like to curse our children with their false prophecies, watch and expect them to be put in jail, die of some evil activities, or simply go insane as a result of frustration.

Many wicked individuals had over the centuries and to this day had helped to facilitate destruction of many of these vulnerable of society. This "***expected end***" He is referring to is: (A) End of abuse in its many forms. That life of abuse, that dark place, must come to an end for your light to shine. The end result our Creator wants for your children is a life of peace, happiness, freedom from abuses, and a close relationship with Him. (B) Influences of evil people and their expectations are nothing good. They simply want to protect their own turf by demanding you live in your wallow mess of abuse, not to succeed and die.

A "*future and a hope*" Your children are to expect eternal life He promised and live on the Earth made new where no oppression will exist, and to succeed in this life with no abuse before He returns.

What did you expect? In the abusive home environment you and your children were like flowers in the attic without a sunray of hope. He must remove you and put you out in the open where His showers of love and sunrays can shine on you. Out there—in the open where you are nurtured by His love through people to care about you. You need new location and new soil to be planted in where your roots will be watered, grow deeply, nourished and maintained through love and encouragement.

Our Heavenly Father wants our children to be amazed of His love for them and to see the difference from where they were, where they are now, and where they can be when they are guided the right way to spread their wings in His bright sunshine and grow right regardless of the normal struggles of life.

A long line of children after you. The long line of children our Creator wants you to expect: children after His character. To live in abusive situations is to cut your life and your future generations short. People are like plants needing good care. Left on its own it will not grow, nor come to its full potential. That is us and our children.

If you want an injured plant to heal and grow beautifully, it must be removed from the poor soil, its roots and stems trimmed and washed. Then transplant it in the good soil and give good nutrition and maintenance.

To grow beautifully you must be transplanted in new and better environment and well cared for. Children after leaving the abusive home if left on their own will not grow healthy without great care. Physically, they may grow, but not to their full potentials. They need lots of support.

During their healing and growing stages they may not always like you but do your best to show o them correct love daily. You are literally untangling that terrible mess of painful tangled neurons that were so painful while living in the abusive home. Much work is needed. Treat them kindly, they are young seedlings need to be treated with tenderness.

They need to be assured of your confidence in providing for them a network of support for continued growth and for in the event you can no longer care for them. This network of support should include loving family and friends; a good place of worship with leaders who are just and through conduct illustrate correct principles; your willingness to lovingly nurture and teach them true principles of life through their growth stages to be permanent in their memory cells to form right character; your willingness and continuous support in helping them identify their potentials and develop their abilities.

The correct principles to govern all areas of our lives are fully illustrated in the Bible and spiritually emphasized in the book of

Proverbs. Children view their parents as their Creator, and rightly so because parents are their only source of nurturing, love, support, security, kindness, first teachers of life, stability, consistency, etc.

These principles of our Creator—directives and commands are intentionally designed to:

1. Help build structure in thoughts, speech, and motor skills.
2. Help build self-confidence and self-esteem when taught properly.
3. Help set standards for life to eliminate flaws in their character and grow maturely.
4. Aids in the automatic time releases of natural hormones (serotonin, dopamine, and norepinephrine) the Creator intentionally put in their DNA from conception to help in their healthy neurological, emotional, mental, physical, and spiritual development for every stages of growth and maturity.

As they grow in their different stages of lives, the automatic time releases of these hormones help them to be ready for different levels of growth and correct mentorships for higher levels of understanding of the principles of life's applications needed for maturity.

1. They begin to correctly perceive instructions—principles taught to them to become permanent in their memory cells to form right character while growing up.
2. These principles continue to activate their DNA after His commands to order their steps in His words. They help the mind and soul to understand the movement of His presence in their lives and in their spirit which will reflect in their actions.
3. Aids them to be emotionally and spiritually ready for one-to-one mentors who are mature leaders of correct principles and instructions to guide them into higher levels of maturity to prevent

them from wearing out physically, emotionally, financially, and spiritually.

4. It aids in the principles of building wealth and how to do business, help to set themselves in order for wealth to pursue them and not them pursuing wealth.
5. Helps them to avoid and discern unclean and clean buildings and people, wise and unwise associations.
6. Higher levels of mentorship aids in recognizing what to study what applies to their anointing (what is revealed of them specifically), and what to have. As they continue to study what applies to their anointing they will use their abilities for good, and to teach others.
7. They learn the correct principles of marriage taught before dating and marriage, to build and develop expectations and characteristics in preparation for marriage before dating. It represents the spiritual maturity they will bring to that special someone.
8. What they learn they will do. Everywhere they go and who they come in contact with they will look and expect to see correct principles of life.

If the parents incorrectly illustrate these principles of life and abuse their children, or live a life of disorder, their maturity stages will be arrested and they will struggle with precarious situations and the consequences that pursue them as they go through life.

Because they see their parents as their Yahweh—their only source of strength and stability, through acts of violence—incest, rape, and other forms of abuses, the automatic time releases of hormones that were intentionally put in place for their correct and timely development will not work in the correct time sequences as programmed in the DNA. Through their early years of development as they begin to understand the principles taught to them, the enemy's plan is to derail their focus. Now through these acts of violence they can become angry, take on all that onto themselves because they lack the skills to correctly process the situations and inflict self-blame, their purposes in life become frustrated, they see rightful authority in the negative, will lack trust in everyone, and will see good leaders in the community as not trustworthy; as a result preventing their maturity.

If the non-abusive parent, other family members and other people in society are not actively and positively involved in the children's lives during the abuse and after the separation the suffering will continue and escalate in worst ways as the child continues to inflict self-blame by taking on everything as guilt into their body, mind, and soul. After an extended period of time it would appear they have become spiritually bipolar—split in the middle as a result of their body, mind, and soul not in sequence/harmony, not growing maturely, the core emotions freezes, become abstinent to proper instructions, and need counseling with clear directives and commands to correct and delete wrong processing of information to help reprogram the neurological system for its correct development and growth.

If non-abusive parents, after the separation/divorce continue with these harmful practices and or adopt new harmful practices, habits, traditions, or lifestyles to teach them; they are been forced to live in two realms—of life and death, working in their bodies. If the negative become stronger then the desire to study and know correct instructions decreases or ceases, they will not be able to identify with the Creator to have joy in their lives to identify their potentials, and they miss their areas of anointing—potentials developing into abilities. The cycle becomes stronger and repeats as they grow and they continue to struggle with harmful situations and terrible consequences in their lives.

OUR HEAVENLY FATHER WANTS US TO PUT A STOP TO ALL THESE EVILS

Our children need to live in peaceful environments to be wholesome. Immediately after taking them out of the abusive environments we need to help switch their mindset from the abusive ways that causes destruction, and help bring them to complete healing, restoration, and peace.

They need peace, love, and clear directives and commands—correct principles and instructions to live in the realm of life where they were created to be for proper growth and prosperity. These principles will aid in: rewiring the brain and spirit to produce stability and consistency; to know structure; and guide them in right connection to Him from which everything flows in their life if they remain in it; they will become more focused in their purpose of understanding His ways and life; helps to unlock the time released capsules of hormones for right growth to begin. Their walk will show continuous healing as their posture will be corrected.

If the process is aborted they freeze in their desire to know themselves in our Creator, worship only and become stuck in the academia of religion without its correct applications in not identifying their true potentials, or seek others to emulate and their lives become frustrated. As a result of this imbalance in their lives they will develop growing closets—difficult areas of life nurtured for withdrawing from His principles and life. Example: addictions to emotions and do not study, addictions to harmful people and things which prevents them from becoming and staying stable, addictions to prayer only without applications to their lives for growth because they are wired incorrectly and stuck half way in their maturity but growing physically only, and develop dependency to other forms of addictions.

Fighting for your children's mind to heal and grow in our Creator's character and to prosper is not an easy task. You will experience attacks ridicule and put downs from other sources that can be very deadly. There are times you must defend them against others in the community by counteracting their cleverly crafted lies with our Creator's words. By doing this you are teaching your children they are valuable and how to stand up for themselves in truth. Do not think because you left the abuser the enemy is not after you. It is on your heels now with more revenge and will target the weaker ones—the children's minds. Pray much and ask the Good Sovereign Heavenly Father to preserve and guide them daily while instructing them rightly.

Before and after leaving your Egypt never treat them as a burden or in your way. While fighting for their souls we must, I repeat, must on a daily basis exercise true forgiveness. Never repeat hurtful topics unless it is in pleasant reflections to help guide them rightly. They fall easily into despair when they do not experience hope and true forgiveness from you. You are their only hope to ever experience true healthy living. Be firm, kind, and patient in the endless hope of good results.

While experiencing healing guard your life and home from evil individuals who are very insensitive to family and community cohesiveness which contributed greatly to your successful healing process. While my son was very young, only starting high school, some parents were telling me it is time for him move out and live on his own while their adult children were still living in their homes with them. Those people we do not acknowledge anymore.

The intercultural expectations often imposed on us can sometimes be a burden for anyone who experienced abuse. Sure it is good to respect all people even when you cannot tolerate their evil behavior. However, some are expecting you to be subjected to them to answer their cruel probing inquiries. Do your best to avoid them or to respectfully decline in your responses and keep moving. Most people do not mean any harm and are only expressing genuine concerns. However, some are deliberately cruel and bound for hell, because that is the route they chose and are plagues and pestilence to be avoided at all cost away from you and you children.

Often times we do not realize it, but our children experiencing such agony can easily fall into despair. The enemy of our souls seeks to destroy their minds while in such delicate state. After it destroys their hope, it possesses and destroys them. Do not give space to it. They are in a confused state and they can easily go the wrong way, and life can easily go wrong for them. We must plead for their souls and ask our Creator, master of the universe to hold unto them for dear life and never let them go.

Do not allow anyone to interfere with their continuous progress in life. Your responsibility is to guide and protect them. When you take this stand your children will learn they are valuable, and to be good parents to others and their own children in the future.

If at all possible help them to find the right group of worship where they will hear the true instructions of our Creator explained in its true context to help give them continued stability, growth, and joy. As they continue to experience healing on all levels they will not be afraid to worship Him.

Connect them with good family members and friends to help build a strong and healthy network of support for their continuous healing and growth. After leaving our Egypt I continually for years make sure my son spend time with family near and far. I sent him long distance on his own for family time to help stay connected with them. For the first time he met family members he never knew and he was well loved. He was not afraid to travel on his own, he loved it.

We are instructed to bless our children. This powerful blessing was given to help heal the mind of the multitude of slaves of their pain and the painful memories of abuse they endured in Egypt, and of the many challenges they will face en route to their homeland and while living there.

Numbers 6:24–27 *"May God bless you and keep you; may God make His face shine on you and show you his favor. May God lift up His face toward you and give you peace."*

This is to be pronounced over them as a reminder that the Sovereign Heavenly Father, our Creator still rules in their lives and always will be with them.

It is not a magic spell to heal them overnight but a promise that He will do all that for them. This is how I often bless my son and he expects it daily. Do this for your children to help them trust to walk in His ways.

Our children are to live in peaceful homes and communities, and to experience peace in all areas of their lives. He will not hide their success but do it openly for all to see. He wants those liars who stood afar off falsely prophesying against our children to see that they are His beloved whom He created, is well pleased and desires them to be successes regardless of parentage and circumstances, and is not happy with those who desires their destruction. When you refuse to adapt to the negative opinions, refuse to continue in the evils that bring destruction on you and your children and others around you and begin to learn and correctly teach and illustrate to your children His principles, He will make them a blessing to you and your community.

Chapter twenty-five

RAGE INTO JOY

Proverbs ***14:10: The heart knows its own sorrows and no one intermeddles with its joy.***

Biblecommenter.com. Matthew Henry's Whole Bible Commentary. This agrees with 1 Co. 2:11: *What man knows the things of a man, and the changes of his temper, save the spirit of a man? 1. Every man feels most from his own burden, especially that which is a burden upon the spirits, for that is commonly concealed and the sufferer keeps it to himself. We must not censure the griefs of others, for we know not what they feel; their stroke perhaps is heavier than their groaning. 2. Many enjoy a secret pleasure, especially in divine consolations, which others are not aware of, much less are sharers in; and, as the sorrows of a penitent, so the joys of a believer are such as a stranger does not intermeddle with and therefore is no competent judge of.*

2 Timothy 1:7: "For God had not given us a spirit of fear, but of power, love, and of a sound mind."

The anger I mentioned before may never totally go away. Even today been aware of my healing process, there are people who know my past situation, and love to keep the memory of the abuser alive, as though I have a responsibility to always think about him.

One lady in particular, may she rest in peace, loves to pretend she cares about that abuser so much, would ask whenever I see her: "How is your ex-husband, have you seen him? Do you not try to keep in touch with him to see if he is okay? What if something happens to him?"

Fortunately for me Yahweh had calmed me down significantly, and also due to respect for her I answered with a quiet no. She often expressed her responsibility of keeping in touch with her vicious and psychotic ex-abuser. I do not see the benefit in that. Once an abuser is out of my life they must stay out forever especially for the reason we had to leave. They are to be avoided at all cost.

It is through these times you will realize you are healing and your anger is been replaced by something else. Make no mistake there will always be a healthy amount of anger still left inside you for self-preservation. It serves as a reminder of where you were, what happened to you, how you left, and where not to return. I tried to rehearse what I would say and how I would react if I would see that abuser. It is never pretty. Therefore, I realize I must continuously ask for help to remember that vengeance is not my responsibility, but our Heavenly Father's. I begged Him to shield us in His Almighty Shadow so that the abuser will never find us nor interfere with us where ever we are, together or alone.

It may seem the anger may never go away, and in part may never all together go away. There is no such thing as forgive and forget. That sentence as a whole is not true. You can forgive, but to forget is humanly impossible. You may forget for a brief moment what you have been through but it will always be in your memory. That is why processing it correctly is an imperative. Having counselors/ mentors and friends who have common sense will help you to see things in better perspective. You may never fully understand in this life why and what you and your children have experienced, and the perpetrator is still alive walking around kicking up the heels joyously. But you will be able to resolve in your soul that what has happened to you and your children was evil.

YaHoshua's intense focus was of great benefit to me. His focus was for our benefit in saving us. He could not afford for one second during torture to retaliate or He would lose us forever. Our survival depended on it.

There is a sense of urgency that surround us—the care of the children, and the injustices that surround them. Before and after leaving an abusive home there is great work in helping our children and we cannot afford to stay angry but must resolve in our soul that our children are our most urgent important focus.

It is healthy to feel revengeful and who would not coming from your situation. No one should escape punishment after doing such crimes. I know the revenge I had in mind cannot come close to what our Creator and time will do to him, nor would it be enough to satisfy me, so I leave it alone. Remembering has its purpose, to help guard you—body, mind, and soul. It will help you to be careful in how you enter other relationships, and how to have healthy relationships.

Another time I had the misfortune of meeting up with the abuser. I was visiting another church and he saw me. He had approached me with his anger. As he approached me his eyes became black as night, and had his hand raised ready to strike me. I told him, "Turn around and go back to hell where you come from." He continued to approach me ready to strike me, and my friend's husband stood up to him, stood between me and the abuser and stopped him in his tracks with a posture of authority. The abuser was shocked and immediately turned around and ran out the church building.

OKAY. It is evident I still have some rage. And I still need some serious counseling. That is okay. The rage in me proved my purpose. I looked back and realized I did not sin in church, even though I really wanted to say other things. That was a victory for me to look him in the face, talk to him boldly, and defend myself. I felt I had to because twenty-four hours a day he was evil to us. I know this conversation with him, if allowed, would not go well for me. And I would not allow him to hurt me in publicly or privately.

It is very clear. You must arm yourself to the teeth with words of power to resist the devil and it will flee from you. Make no mistake the devil and the abuser does not like you and no amount of friendship with them will help you. Revenge is in their minds and repentance does not exist in their minds. I refuse to waste time in sackcloth and ashes to pray for him. I mostly pray for me and my son's protection, and for our Heavenly father to keep the abuser from us as far as the east is from the west.

When you refuse to discuss the abuser people do not understand how deep your wounds are, and how each time they mentioned the abuser they are trying to keep the hurt raw. They are most times extremely insensitive asking about the abuser in your children's presence knowing what they endured. They do not care.

Others may want to identify you with the abuser as though you are still intimate, when your intention is to heal and move on. Most do not mean harm. Many are confused as to why you are walking upright as though you were never hurt, looking blessed, which means to them either nothing happened to you and you left for nothing, or you were the one doing the abusing. Choose not to care about their words. They are in their own world with it. They simply do not understand the healing balm of Gilead and His power to save.

Through these painful trials I am comforted by David's words in *Psalms 3, "Many are they increase that trouble me, many are they that rise up against me, many are they who say of my soul 'there is no help for him in God."* This they often forget. *"But you, O Lord, are a shield for me, my Glory and the One who lifts up my head. I cried to the Lord with my voice, and He heard me from His holy hill. I lay down and slept, I awoke, for the Lord sustained me. I will not be afraid of ten thousands of people who have set themselves against me all around."*

They can be very intimidating, but refuse to allow them to take precedence over your life, and your goal to heal and successfully move on. Those who care will behave differently toward you and your children.

I know my personality may not reflect a believer in our Creator, but He is still working with me. You must stand up for your rights: your responsibilities to be His child you were created to be, to lovingly care for your children, and to be of great benefit to mankind, and many more. I do not know what challenges you will face in life but make no mistake you will get them, different for everyone and with varying degrees. He did not bring you out to become coward. Out here away from the abuser you are free and safe to stand knowing help is available to you and your children.

Paul too experienced mockery and scorn in his trials, and in his efforts to encourage the believer he expressed in ***Romans 8:38–39;*** *"For I am convinced that neither death nor life, neither angels nor demons, neither the present nor future, not any powers, 39: neither heights nor depth, nor anything else in all creation, will be able to separate us from the love of* our Creator *that is in* our Messiah, *YaHoshua our Lord."*

He makes it plain to everyone that nothing they do to you, no amount of jeering or scorning will ever stop our Creator from loving you.

Does this sound like I am encouraging you to be at war with the enemy? You are correct. Not a physical or verbal war, if not necessary, but to take a stand knowing the difference between what He says He will do for you and what these negative people are telling you causing you to feel hurt repeatedly.

When you were in the abusive home, you were kept down in every way. You were a prisoner of war. The enemy was at war against you and for a while its demons and servant abuser had the upper hand. That was designed to shut you up from reasoning and praising our Creator, and you were to die. You had no clue what David meant when he said: ***"The joy of the Lord is your strength."*** In your darkness of time, you probably asked "What joy, what strength." How could such sorrow be turned into joy? It may be difficult to understand that you will ever get out never mind recovering to have joy. But in every war the end must come. As sure as the sun will shine tomorrow it will pass. It too will pass. It must end.

Now you are out of your abusive home. That is one thing to be happy about. The rage, anger, hostility, and revenge that were all built up inside of you may start to manifest. Recognize it for what it is. Know that such prolonged feelings of rage if allowed to be nurtured inside of you will only cause much mental instability and illnesses later and will only prove to retard you and your children's healing progress. Quickly get all the help you can while you are in this state and allow Him to work with you.

Knowing He is with you is a start. But you must daily surrender all these feelings to Him. Continue to ask Him to take them away and replace them with correct instructions. You cannot do this on your own without His help. Ask Him to forgive you for everything you may have done wrong, whether you are aware of them or not. The anger you also expressed to your children when you felt angry ask them forgiveness. They may sometimes not believe you because of the level and frequency of rage you may have expressed but keep trying and show them you are trying.

It is not correct to say you must forget what had happened and move on. Please be real with yourself and life. If people choose to forget then they are blatantly saying that it never happened and, or it may have been their own fault. You are not trying to remember it as a memorial of what a scoundrel the abuser was, or to keep weeping over your victimization. To forget is also to dismiss the responsibility of the abuser, and also yours. Your responsibility is to learn from it and move on positively with your life to help others. Take full advantage of freedom to study His words and talk with Him.

People often say that you can by yourself dismiss the evil thoughts of revenge inside your whole being. No, it is not correct. It is only by fervently asking Him to remove those situations from inside of you, they will be replaced with His peace, and you will gain the victory. He will remove them and forgive you of them as well. You will be surprised that He immediately does it.

You are not trying to be healed to be a better person for the abuser to like you. Who cares what they like. Do you not know when you were beautiful they did not like you? They distressed you greatly and hated you more. What makes you think they will like you now that you are glowing?

I was escorted to an event and knew I was healing and beginning to look different and feeling more confident. People were excited to see me, but I was looked on with rage by those who hated me. Their statistics say that I should be suffering, starving, naked, and going crazy. Yet there I was with the audacity to dress and look good, and best of all I am in my sound mind, and feeling too blessed to even care about the past or what they were thinking of me and my son.

Allow yourself to be healed. YaHoshua did not die for nothing. He knew what His mission was; to heal you, to deliver you out of the enemy's territory, release the captives held prisoner to the vices and power of the abuser design for you. Your roots will grow deep into truths, replacing all the lies that the abuser and wicked people in society have been feeding you to give you depression.

You need to be in the right place to get help to rebuild your life and repair old family relationships that were shut out and regenerate numerous generations to come by seeing your children been healed as well. People will see that He did deliver you and you are not wasting away as they expected and they too will have hope. They will see how you and your children are been raised up to stand on mountains and walk on stormy seas. There will be stormy times in your lives but you will not sink. You will learn to overcome it all, look brighter, walk better, your posture will be straight, and your speech will be different.

Make no mistake our Creator hates injustices and the praises of an abuser. He will cause your efforts to be established in truth and renew His covenant with you and your children. An abusive home is a place of disorder which does not reflect correct principles to live out in your life as is intended. Work with Him here. Do not disappoint Him. He wants to be proud of you. He is proud of you already for calling out to Him for help and for trusting Him.

Now He wants to show you off. People who stood afar off, and even in your face mocked you in your despair saying there is no help for you, are about to have a rude awakening. Others whose heart mourned for you will see the salvation of the true Messiah in your life. You are walking testimonies to His answers to their prayers. They will now see you glowing and everything you wear will be beautiful on you. People will recognize you now for who you should have been all along.

When you were married, you should have looked beautiful, glowing and growing in the light of our Heavenly Father and all areas of your life a success. Instead the abuser wanted you to be a dried up twig. They will look at you and see you been replenished, health will begin to renew, as a desert flower that blooms in the time of rain. Even some of the religious leaders who once scorned us were surprised to see that their prophecies against us failed, and are angry.

He will not bring you this far to leave you to dry up and die as they prophesied. Remember ***Psalm 23:1–3*** "*The Lord is my Shepherd; I shall want nothing. He makes me lie down in green pastures, and leads me beside the waters of peace; he renews life within me and for his name's sake guides me in the right path.*"

He will be your peace and provider; and you will never again desire an abuser nor stay in any harmful relationships. You can resist any potential intimate relationship that is not healthy. He will bring you to a place where your soul will be cleansed, healed, and refreshed, and to have that *ah* moment that will last forever. You will look back and be amazed at how each day is a new beginning. Most importantly your sins are forgiven and you have a clean start with Him in life.

Chapter twenty-six

YOUR GIFTS

The Heavenly Father blessed me with many gifts before marriage, one of which was art. I loved art and did many pieces for people who knew me. The abuser also did art but was constantly degrading my work. For the years of marriage I did none. My talents were so greatly suppressed that I could not even start any. Immediately after leaving my art enthusiasm was returned with a passion. My son and I did our first set of paintings to decorate our new home. We continued doing huge ones, framed them and now they graced our home. I was blessed to do other paintings for individuals who paid me for my work and are still enjoying them, and I also enjoyed them when I visit their homes. When people come to our home they are blessed by our art. My son also did some himself which are now displayed in our new home.

I also enjoyed gardening before marriage and with permission from the property manager every square inch of grass of my front yard was removed and replaced by plants and flowers. The first year I did this I won the Community in Bloom awards, Five Blooms in total—Three Blooms award for the best garden on our street. I also won Two Blooms from the region's office for the garden facing the main street near the property manager's office.

Be thankful to our Creator always. Your small gifts can become larger, and the big ones can become more perfected when you research and work on them. Be excited about them. They are part of you He gave you to bless your family and others. Whatever the size of your budget you can accomplish it. Enjoy looking at many home magazines, visit fabric stores and feel the textures of each fabric and let your imagination soar.

I also enjoyed decorating and would spend much time in libraries looking at home and garden magazines for decorating ideas, dreaming of beautifully decorating my new home, and of been hospitable again. People are surprised of the simplicity and beauty of our home. I do not see it and often only see large room for improvement. But I know they are been honest and I am thankful to them.

Successes for most people are limited to huge accomplishments only and may want to impose them on you as the only proof of success. For us success began when we left the abusive home, staying close with our Heavenly Father, healing daily, watch our garden grow, having the freedom to decorate and light our own candles as we please, and the freedom to explore access to continuing our educational pursuits, gainful employment, freedom to improve relationships with family and friends.

For a while I was forced to slow down receive more treatments to heal properly. Rushing into a full load of school activities with long distance traveling each day to school proved to be harmful at that time.

If you cannot achieve your goals one way, there are other ways to achieve them rightly. Equally important is to enjoy the other gifts you have. They will brighten your life and give you hope to carry on.

Another gift in life I enjoyed tremendously before marriage was hospitality. I enjoyed having people over my home most weekends for dinner, potlucks, and sleepovers, and even random visits from family and friends were welcomed. I loved that kind of fellowship. It nurtured us tremendously.

Soon after we moved and got some furniture, it was back in our life. Sometimes we slowed down, but we can always have it anytime we want. I allowed this to prevent feelings of abandonment and isolation, and to be part of our healing. When we are not having lunch at our home we are at someone's home. Sometimes we slow down, that is okay too.

While you are waiting for your children to mature and be on their own, teach them to be thankful each day for their gifts and interests, and show them how to decorate their life with their own talents, and do the good things that will help them to grow and be happy while healing.

These finer things in life cannot be replaced. They need to be nurtured. Try and remember the good things you enjoyed doing, what you would love to do, and go for it. If you cannot remember, your friends and family will help you to identify your talents.

These also apply to your children. Look for activities that they enjoyed and help them to research and attend. Never block their interests in activities that are good, although different from your own interests. They have different dreams that may not be compatible with your life goals. Realize that each activities, which may not lead to that top paying career you so desire for them will help lead to great quality lives. For example, skydiving, art, music, camping, swimming, photography, home decorating, painting, woodworking, needlecraft, gardening, snowshoeing, skiing, traveling, archery, and many more can help them to have very healthy lives. These are only some of the many activities that are very healthy and healing to their minds. When they are bored with school or with everyday life they will always have some healthy activities to resort to pass the time, or if they choose to develop into their own careers. These will bring happiness in their relationships with friends, family, and their own intimate family in the future.

Your new community may have host of activities to attend. Many recreation centers may have at least one activity you can enjoy and afford and can find great success in learning one at a time. If they seem not interested, try and get them excited about something. Travel with them to visit different places such as: the zoo, winter sports, Olympic sports, music bands, concerts, art exhibits, and different activities that your community centers may have. Take them to their friend's activities to see if they would like it.

Encourage your children to interact with children of other cultures within these activities, if possible. If you have hatred against other cultures it will only hinder your new growth experiences in healing and your relationship with The Sovereign Creator. This is the time to explore the different experiences that you need to have a better quality life. Your children need these experiences with people of different cultures who have the same needs. You will be wonderfully amazed at their testimonies of how they have overcome what you have endured and possibly worst. They too have challenges with their children and are trying as you are. Their challenges are different in degrees but challenges all the same. Some have been hurt by separation from parents, family, and have endured hardships that may cause you to weep and count your blessings.

You are free to make mistakes. Sometimes you may try something without great success. That is okay. These are your own mistakes. Enjoy them with a heart of thankfulness to our Creator.

Chapter twenty-seven

GO LIGHT YOUR WORLD

You may never believe at this point in your growth that your life could ever be an example for others. After you leave this abusive home you may plan to keep to yourself thinking you will never get hurt again. Well, think again. As long as the devil and its host of fallen angels are not burning in hell, there will always be the occasional tough times in everyone's life. No one is too nice, educated, too important, or too beautiful to experience pain.

After we left we were very careful who we allowed in our lives and still are, while helping others to be happy. Our Heavenly Father did not bring us this far to not reach out to others. We cannot know for sure how, or how others watching are learning about Him. Yet it does happen. When you begin and continue to grow you cannot help but shine while going through the healing process. You will be a walking example of what it is to be taken out of a dark place and now shining.

People in your environment will be astonished to see you and your children looking better each day and growing healthy. They may never know the details of what you have endured if you never tell them. However, these people monitor your growth, because they correctly perceived your difficulties and prayed for you.

People do groan in their spirit on your behalf without telling you and experience relief when they see improvements in your life. Example: When my son and I first moved in our new home, we lived very far from the nearest grocery story. We did not have a vehicle at the time and we struggled with grocery in our weakened condition. After we received our first vehicle, one neighbor walked past me in my garden and exclaimed; "You finally got a car." She had said it with such empathy I almost cried. I realized she too had felt our sorrows and now feel relieve that we will be ok.

I frequently meet people who are experiencing what we left behind, some more intense, pain is pain whatever the source. I was able to share with some individuals our deliverance and how all the material things we left behind were replaced with better things. People whom we met reached out to us in love to provide us with many good things and in the space of four months living there our totally empty space was transformed to a beautiful furnished home. It would not have made sense to carry all those good-for-nothing things with us. We are very grateful to them. Every item in our home has a story of love.

I was told our new home was once a place of violence with previous residents. Our neighbors were shocked to see the overall transformation that had taken place inside the home and the gardens and feel safe since we moved in. While listening to their story, I had difficulty understanding what those former residents had experienced.

However, after reflecting on our own past experiences and what we have left behind, it is not difficult to imagine how much more intense the experiences were not only for those past residents been victims of abuse, but also for those who witnessed it and were impacted by it.

Abuse is not a private affair. All individuals in our mile radius and beyond are affected by it. They also live in fear. If you choose to stay in your abusive life, you are also subjecting others to your life of violence. These neighbors shared with us some of the horrible experiences they have witnessed of the previous residents. They too were terribly impacted by his cruelties to his family and his violent behavior to people in the community.

The neighbors suffered also because the abused spouse refused to accept help. They expressed grave concern for her and the children's safety due to his open hostility toward them and how the atmosphere in the neighborhood was filled with fear. She outwardly expressed fear of the abuser, yet refused to accept the help offered. After a while she began to exhibit behavioral signs of mental illness.

An abuser is not violent to one individual but to all. The violence may be expressed in different degrees, but violence all the same. I understand what they mean because I too am quite wary of people who are violent and unfaithful to their spouse. Their heart will not be clean toward you, and they are in fact always looking for an open door in your life to abuse you too.

In your new freedom you will meet individuals who may want to treat you like that, do not allow anyone to exercise such displaced behavior over you and get away with it. Get the right help to deal with it swiftly and appropriately. It will empower you to continue to live free in this newfound freedom our Creator has given you to establish his character and presence in you.

They may not like you standing up against their behavior but that is not your problem. The message here:

It is not important they like you, nor the message
that they must stop, but they must get it.

The Bible tells us that in the last days before Christ returns more abusers will exist. ***Second Timothy 3:1–3***: "*You must face the fact; the final age of this world is to be a time of troubles. Men will love nothing but money and self; they will be arrogant, boastful, and abusive; with no respect for parents, no gratitude, no pity, no natural affection; they will be implacable in their hatreds, scandal mongers, intemperate and* *fierce, strangers to all goodness, traitors, adventurers, swollen with self-importance."*

Also in **Ephesians chapter 6,** Paul encourages us to learn of our Creator, make sure we are growing in His character and His word so we will be able to stand in these last days.

He does not want us to be afraid. He said: ***2 Timothy 1:7***—*"For God has not given us a spirit of fear, but of power and of love and of a sound mind."*

To stand means: to resolve in your soul to maintain a strong unchangeable conviction in His principles to resist all evils that will come toward you and others while you are alive. Speak up and take all the right necessary actions against it. Count the cost in all things: stand vs. not to stand. When you stand, the abuser will not like you. But that is not your focus. The abuse must stop. They will not like you standing up, and may use their position of authority to get away with it and perhaps try other ways to hurt you, but stand you must.

The abuser may try to abuse others out of retaliation against you resisting them, but they are simply looking for new victims. Some will come after you in other ways because they fail in their attempts to control you. When everyone stands against it eventually the abuser must one day stop.

The more you stand the less hurt to contain in your soul, your spirit will remain free and clean, and will become stronger and more educated to counteract each attack.

Taking a stand against evil does not mean you have had such experiences; but you have the strong conviction in your soul that the evil actions are contradictory to what the presence of our Creator represents in you, against the law, against His principles and the possible outcome if allowed to continue.

If you do not stand, in short, everyone could be in grave danger.

In my experiences with abusive people, this is what they taught me: abusers do not like to be judged, and they will tell you that. However, when a person mistreats you this is what they do: (1) They give you front row seats to their performance to see up close not only their behavior, what precipitated it, but also how it affects you. (2) They give you the authority, power, and permission to judge and condemn their actions and character.

Judging is the ability to discern the difference between wrong and right, and ability to condemn wrong actions not the person. To say you have no right to discern if they were wrong or right in their behavior is saying you should have no knowledge of their intent and motive of their ill dispositions and of the growing darkness inside them toward you and were to be their doormat. They themselves know they are wrong, and will often times use their positions of authority in the community to block and oppress you, and to quash your own authority against such behavior.

You must grow. If you do not, you would be no better off than been left in the abusive home to die. You do not need to be a doctor nor an educated person to understand what I mean.

My friend Neses was extremely abused by her husband when I met her. I shared with her some messages of hope were given me, now for her. She was strengthened to leave the abuser, got medical help to start her healing processes, got counseling to understand her needs, and learned to walk away from the material things that did not matter. She learned that things are replaceable, she is not.

Many victims are fearful of moving on with their own lives. For a long time their life was enshrouded in darkness, not what the Creator intended. Now they are in the wide open with no apparent guide. Teach them that it is possible and important to be happy again been single because they can acquire all the right skills to live a life of good quality. When you are happy you will be more mature in your discernment in all relationships.

The good news the Creator wants you to share is the message of deliverance, hope, and restoration for His children. It is not necessary to share all the details of your abuse as it most times proved to intensify your pain and the pain of your hearers who are experiencing their own distress. It was not good to have experienced this, nor was even necessary. But because of His grace while in it He lifted us out of it, clean us up, and make us shine.

Many people despair been victims of abuse. They are deeply embarrassed of it and some are re-victimized by others in society. Many do not have a voice and suffer deeply. I was very happy to help my friend Neses. She got hope and courage to do the right thing.

If you have experienced abuse and have left, do not speak evil of anyone still experiencing it. Can leaving such violence and experiencing such love of the Heavenly Father cause us to look down on others? No, it does not. As a result of such experience we should be more loving and intelligent to not refuse to help others who are walking the same road we once walked. We can help them walk it more easily and recover more quickly. They too now are going through their Egypt similar to yours. They need our help.

If you have escaped such a dark place at the time of reading this book, remember how you groaned in your spirit during those years of abuse inflicted on you and your children, how you had entered your Egypt, how it was transformed from what appeared to be good to bad, and how He touched the hearts of individuals to intercede for your deliverance. Remember how you were shown your Red Sea and were instructed to step in for Him to part it for you. Remember the loving individuals who helped you along the way. Look where you are now. To turn your back on other victims whom He show you is to imply that we have only physically left our Egypt. We must leave our Egypt in every way, to never return for anything, nor want to see others there.

Some abused individuals who have not left their abusive life, had the audacity to look down on other single individuals who have no spouse, compared themselves against them, and surmised that they still been married and abused, are better off. How shocking to think that having an abusive spouse is better than having none at all. These people may have at some time were shown their Red Sea, refused to step in for escape, and now may never able to leave alive.

Many others have a conscience and may never have experienced such a place can easily be empathetic because we all have a friend, enemy, neighbor, family member, and other people in society who were injured in this place. It is not a nice place to be.

When you think of all you experienced in your Egypt and your suffering while healing you will begin to fully understand what ***Exodus 20:2***, *"I am the Lord your God, who brought you of the land of Egypt, out of the house of bondage."* Be very thankful to Him each day. We are extremely thankful continuously because we did not do it on our own. Remember His love to you, now you are shining because He wants to show you off, do not kick up your heels against Him nor anyone else who supported you.

The entire chapters of **Exodus 20 and 34**, and **Nehemiah chapter 9** can be applied here. He wants you to know that when you leave your Egypt this is how He wants you to shine and continue to shine. He wants to release your entire being from the past by teaching you what you should have learned back there to live a life of good quality. Do not go back to anything or anyone who kept you from His principles designed to heal you.

From **Exodus chapter 20 to Leviticus chapter 27**, our Creator had introduced His seasons of our joy and growth. They are His appointed times to spend with Him and be closer to Him. These instructions are already established on Earth as they were already established in heaven, and have powerful implications on our lives now and for eternity. They cannot be changed by anyone and has powerful influence in every individual lives and on every nation.

Now He wants you to call Him daddy. Remember His words in ***Romans 8:15–16***: "*For you did not receive the spirit of fear of bondage again to fear, but you received the spirit of adoption by whom we cry Abba Father.*" That spirit of fear is the unclean garment of heaviness and of violence that once covered you, He wants to take off you and replace it with the garment of life and praise. That spiritual connection others say you will always have with the abuser will be replaced with His spirit of adoption giving you the right to call Him Father; because He now is in total control of you and your children's life. And He wants to bring you to an expected end—***Jeremiah 29:11***

We did not know His principles before entering an abusive relationship. He is promising to renew His covenant with us when we see our true condition, cry out to Him and seek Him with all our heart and obey Him. He will listen and allow you to be aware of His presence in you and your life, restore you in every way, identify you with Him, and will show you where He intended you to be in your life. You will no longer be connected to the abuser who has no rightful access to you anymore. And they must shut up.

You may ask how He can possibly do this for you and your children. It is simple. ***Philippians 1:6***: "*Been confident of this very thing, that He who started a good work in you will complete it until the day of YaHoshua, our True Messiah.*"

Chapter twenty-eight

YOUR REVIEW

Be thankful with all your heart be curious and desperate to learn all His principles: commandments, laws, statutes, and judgments and apply them to your soul and in every area of your life. Be desperate to have them activated in your DNA to be separated from every trace of attractions that caused you to be enslaved in your Egypt, to not identify with them anymore. This is a lifetime process.

While living out such drama, we often wondered and even feared, "When we leave such darkness, how will we ever know we are doing the right thing, and how do we measure and keep track of our progress?"

Many victims of abuse return to their home of violence, of course the end is rarely good. They returned for fear of growth. Many did not understand the possible consequences before returning.

This fear of growth is very debilitating. Such individuals had forgotten who had taken them out of bondage, and had put them where they could get help to grow and glow with all the sun rays of hope and possibilities.

Deuteronomy chapter 8, Moses had reviewed with the multitude of slaves how our Creator had delivered them from their Egypt and healed them of their past sufferings. The lessons they have learned through the Red Sea and the wilderness experiences surpassed all PHDs you and I could ever achieve. They are now in the wide open where the limits for success are the galaxy stars, with the expected challenges, be thankful and never forget their past and vow to never return. Those experiences were too horrifying for any human to endure, to be avoided at all cost, and not subject anyone to such horrors.

When you leave such an estate as that you are to abhor it with all your body, mind, and soul, never forget it, and never subject anyone else to it. Keep in proper perspective the experiences of the past, where you are now, and our Heavenly Father's ultimate goal for you with Him. It was cruel character that caused your suffering. Now you need His instructions to develop His character to keep you safe.

Often times we will reflect on what He did for us, how He had taken us out in ways we did not realize until years after. When you spend time with Him intimately communicating with Him through your soul, listen intently and patiently to His voice. Allow Him to reason with you through your soul to show you where you went wrong and keep asking Him forgiveness while accepting the roles you may have played in the demise of this relationship. It was a deep cleansing moment He had put me through, so intense I knew I had to listen and ask forgiveness and help of each revelation. It is not a time to argue back, nor is it a time of self-blame. It is the reality of the situation—you were not mature enough nor close enough to Him to even reconsider entering such an awful estate.

Today, we continue to see the humor; the intensity; and the fierceness in which He worked to protect, deliver and preserve us body, mind, and soul. It is not to be taken lightly. This is not something He wishes to repeat because of our willfulness to return to the abuser or to another one. He did not take you out, clean and polish you up to return to that dark place, that vacuum air of darkness. It is a deep pit with no bottom. How do you expect to shine there?

To return is proving to the abusers that they are right in what they did. They will only become more treacherous toward you and will never accept accountability and responsibility for their own actions.

Friends, family, and people in your new circles will help you review your growth. Often times that may not be enough, or you have no one to help measure your improvements. Ask a counselor or someone you trust. I too often wondered. Our Heavenly Father talks to me in dreams that are so amazing sometimes I need to pray and meditate much to understand. This is one of His ways of communicating with me. He will show you things too. You are His child and want you hurt no more. He speaks in plain language that you will understand. We translate them into parables to make them into our own story which causes His messages to be unclear creating for ourselves difficulties in life. This is my dream:

My son and I accompanied by other individuals in this dark room. We were traveling, flying parallel to the ground. The storm was horrible. We approached the edge of what appeared to be Niagara Falls and were carried over it. The water was as black tar and raging violently. At times we almost skimmed the surface and were afraid we would be taken away. Yet we traveled over. The sky was as black as tar and the storm was horrifying. We continued across and suddenly taken up, up, and traveling upward. There we entered what appeared to be separate class rooms. We were presented to our own classrooms by separate teachers who were already there with other students. As my son was seated he immediately he got a call from a friend who was in deep sorrow. He wept bitterly for this friend, because he encouraged him several times, and now it seems his friend was in deep despair and wanted to give up on life.

When I awoke I instantly knew our Heavenly Father was reviewing with us what we were taken from and where we were at the moment.

He had promised that when the waters come, it will not overflow us. He did not allow the trials of life to destroy us. The water in my dream represented the troubles, trials, persecution, abuses we had endured, call it what you may it was more than humanly bearable. Yet He was stronger than all the storms that will come in your life. My son at the time of the dream was very troubled by a friend who was in deep sorrow. He constantly did his best to communicate and support him. We both had our own goals to pursue which we successfully did.

Chapter twenty-nine

CONCLUSION

Today, many views exist on marriage and companionship. How to endure the hardships of an abusive relationship is subject to different opinions, interpretation of one's own life experiences and our Creator's principles. Many live in their own perfect world and choose to pretend such violence does not exist in the universe, and if it does the victims are blamed for lacking the wisdom to see beyond the violence to accept and love the "perceived" good in the abuser, or should have the skills to stop the violence against them.

Many marriages exist today with daily conflicts and its absence means something is wrong. It is not important what society considers normal. What is important is a healthy relationship with our Creator flowing outwards to people.

Healthy and happy marriages do exist, is not a figment of your imagination. There are couples who do not live at variance with each other and all the unnecessary drama. They truly love and respect each other.

Yet, there are marriage seminars teaching couples how to cope with each other's ill compatibilities and how to communicate to avoid an explosive situation.

This is the mental health of a victim been held hostage by an abductor, living in fear, and always walking on egg shells to avoid unintended and unexpected explosions. The human mind can never be conditioned to live harmoniously with an abuser.

Because we are all impacted to some degree by the existence of abuse and its different facets, accepting the call to His grace to correct all wrong values, and the expectation and responsibility to have available to oneself the freedom for healing and growth is an imperative.

Years ago at a round table group family seminar, a counselor spoke. He had this air-brained-scheme that daily conflicts—quarrels, distress, are normal in a marriage. Most counselors present at the meeting disagreed with his statements and tried to correct him in explaining that living with such conflicts been referred to, is unhealthy. There should be no reason for this continuous distress in the home. He ignored them and persisted in his theory by using his position of authority insisting we believe and accept everything he says, and we are not to think or ask questions for ourselves.

Webster's Dictionary defines:

Conflict *n.—struggle, trial of strength, variance*
v.t.*—to be at odds with inconsistent with, clash, strike*

This word is often wrongly used to describe everyday healthy communications on all levels in their lives, and its misapplications often give license to abusers to inflict distresses in every way onto others, and especially to their intimate partner. Conflict is neither disagreement nor argument.

The word *argument* is derived from the word *argue.*

Webster's Dictionary defines:

Argue *v.t., prove, offer reasons, dispute*
v.t.—prove by reasoning; discuss

The word *disagreement* is an antonym of the above derived from the word *agree.*

Webster's Dictionary defines:

Agree, *v.t.: be of one mind; consent; harmonize; determine, settle*

Differences in opinions are not conflict. Disagreements can clearly be discussed with reasoning, clarity of mind, and thought. Arguments are only different thoughts expressed by each individual in approaching any topics. One like orange, the other likes grapes for their own reasons, for example. Nothing wrong in this, yet workable when combined.

In these definitions it is clear that although some differences in opinions will exist, and some may not bond together. The goal is to peacefully and amicably discuss something with consent, even though an agreement may not be reached at the time of discussion.

Conflicts come when disagreement escalates into struggle of the will and individuals are using their feelings to control the other resorting to disrespect during an argument/disagreement, the real issue is often forgotten and lost; now arises an emotional crisis accompanied by fierce personalities clashing against each other—this is now the real issue, hard to deal with. And reasoning is not allowed here unless one partner either give up their autonomy, or walks away.

Conflict is numbing to the nerves and nullifies the brain any time of the day, month, year you experience it. Imagine experiencing this every day in your relationships. It is worse than having screaming teenagers in your house.

The counselors asked him if living in such daily conflicts referred to is healthy for the children. He tried to avoid them by looking around for a response to determine if the questions should be respected.

I was expecting him to at least answer that question regarding the mental health of children living in such daily conflict. I expressed to him I needed an answer to that question because I had grave concerns regarding such children. One lady in the group had signaled to him I was mentally ill.

He responded, "If you believe that daily conflicts, quarrels, and distress in the home are not healthy between married couples, you really need psychiatric evaluation and counseling..." He continued his insults and ended, "I insist after the session you must see me in my office for serious counseling."

Well, after all this stupidity was over and his infamy speech ended, while I was speaking with the other counselors, the same lady who had undermined me to him approached me with the speaker and insisted I go get counseling from him. I took advantage of the group of counselors near me and boldly refused. "No. What do I need counseling from him for? What kind of counseling could he possibly give us, to go home and become belligerent to our families?" The other counselors seeing my reaction and remembering his insults stepped forward and responded in a calm and firm manner with the deliberate intent to give them the message they are not allowed to intimidate me or anyone. They looked horrified and realized they was alone in their false ideas.

Yet there are many individuals who will defend everything said by such individuals. The stupidity of anyone to follow such false leaders blindly, believing every evil thing that comes out of their mouth. The audacity of leaders to think that their education give them authority to teach you lies using such garbage and impose it on others as truth. Teaching such evil doctrines instantly opens the door to a whole host of evil into your homes to use you as target practice of distress until you are dead.

There is no telling what darkness feels like until you allow yourself to be indoctrinated with all this garbage. He was not teaching us how to live a life of good quality. He was imposing on us—compliance, and compliance, to him and his wicked ideas. Had I been the "mentally ill" person he thought, I would have felt pity for myself, and walked into his office like a scared drug addict who needs a quick fix. I would have come out like a senseless individual totally vulnerable to his every whim and false doctrines; as he was to his own grand illusions. They have no clue what abuse is, what it feels like, nor what fuels it. Yet they are here using and imposing their false teachings giving permission to the abuser to fry your nerves on a daily basis.

Experience has proven over the years, that when a person speaks contradictory to correct principles of life, that person is already living a life contrary to correct principles of life and is presenting own false ideas to obtain approval of their wicked intentions.

Abuse is fueled by the spirit of darkness and fear. Its intent is to destroy you in every way. It does not reason with its opponents and your children are the prime targets to cut off their generations of prosperous human beings. There is no reasoning with them.

We have had enough. My son had suffered much, left, and will never reconcile back to the abuser. How much can a child endure? Had we not left I would have lost him to either death, or total nervous breakdown. My only regret was staying in it so long. Our Creator had shown me the damage that was inflicted on him and he needed immediate and complete healing in his body, mind, and soul. We continued with counseling, medical treatments, and physiotherapy and we continued to experience healing in every area of our lives.

When you are in this dark place and leave, do not return there for anything. Your life is in danger. Do not believe it will ever work out. People can say whatever they want, until they have experienced it. Do not allow them to use their misinterpretations of life as authority over you to steer you back there.

When you choose Grace, Grace walks with you. It requires true love of yourself and of others and it does not come without a price: to step out of the known—your Egypt into the unknown—your Red Sea. Stepping into unfamiliar territory is always risky and frightening. It is to leave behind the one you once loved who has become your enemy, and embracing the unknown without duress. Taking that giant leap of faith you will feel the difference and awakening of your true self, and the awareness of what you really should be and is not. You are saying to yourself, your children and the world you are ready to make that change. We start to think and act differently. It will frighten the abuser, but that is not your problem.

In this new path you will have new experiences that come with its own components of fear but not the kind you experienced in the abusive home. This kind of fear is the generator of new respect for life, to have the opportunity to risk changes, failures and successes, and the deep desire to really know what true love is all about.

This is acceptance of the call of Grace—call to awakening, deliverance, restoration, a healthy relationship in Him and with others. It requires a giant leap of faith to mature from spiritual childhood into spiritual adulthood.

Only when you take that giant leap into the unknown of total self-hood, realizing your need for emotional and psychological healing and discovering your unique individuality that you will be free to proceed along higher paths of spiritual growth and express true love in its greatest dimensions.

He is desperate to help you to lift you out of the ashes of your circumstances; to open your eyes and give you courage to see yourself for who you really are – His child, and wants you to experience opportunities to meet new friends, be safe, be beautiful again, and even better than before. It will take work and lots of thinking. But you will be free to think and work without abuse.

His light overcomes all darkness in and around us. These darkness—whether they be negative thoughts, abusive memories, abusive people in our lives, lack of finances, etc., or anything else that blocks you from your potentials and abilities. Ask Him to be in every area of your life. His light will awaken in your soul the desire to be whole, freedom from all that prevents your growth and all the darkness will be gone from your life. He will work with you to root them out. The darkness will never have the mastery over his light in and around you.

When we accept the call of Grace and perceive its reality, our understanding of ourselves as meaningless and insignificant is shattered. You realized that what you previously thought of yourself; to be a truly loveable person, conscientious, intelligent, and all that is good was not a pipe dream.

What you were before you entered this abusive environment, what you have become while in this environment, and what you are in danger of becoming if you do not leave is nothing in comparison to what you can become when you take that giant leap of faith and allow the power of Grace to work for and points you to your spiritual growth is of the upmost importance to something greater than ourselves and that self-proclaimed abuser. You will realize that the abuser has nothing over you, and is nothing in comparison to the One who calls us to Grace.

Enjoy more your close relationship in the Creator. Nurture it each day; because when things and people come and go, His words remain: *"I will never leave you or desert you."* ***(Hebrews 13:5)*** Enjoy your newfound freedom, your progress, new walk with Him, and your children as you watch them grow each day. They will not be with you forever. They will grow up and spread their wings even more and farther.

Plan to be there to help them through the rough times they will face. Be the shoulder they choose to lean, cry, or to laugh on when they need to. Keep your home clean, beautiful, peaceful, and happy; for their safety to live with you while maturing and return to occasionally after they grow up and leave. Help them to hold their head up when times get tough. Encourage them that through Grace we are helped to overcome obstacles in our lives now and in the future, and to know that they are included in this journey. Teach them that success comes in many ways and they will experience it. Enjoy each day of your life with our Heavenly Father as though it is the last and the challenges you face will endure them without duress.

Our Creator's great comfort to us comes in many ways. This is one of them. *Isaiah **41:10:** "Fear nothing, for I am with you, be not afraid, for I am your God, I will strengthen you, I help you, I support you with my victorious right hand."*

If it was not for Grace none of us would be okay. And because of Grace all of us can.

Freedom is a great place to be. You were free and can be free again. Stand courageous. You are His child. You have already won. We have won.

Acknowledgments

TO *our awesome Creator—Yahweh:* Who led us out of our Egypt and through our Red Sea—all honor, thanks, and praise belong to you, always.

To our family members: Many thanks for your great support, friendship, your many prayers, encouragements, humor, and for loving us in your own special ways.

Women's shelter and staff: Thank you and continue to do your great work.

To all our friends: Thank you for your continuous support and love. All of you are correct: anything is better than this.

To all religious leaders, and counselors in our communities who are doing their best: Thank you for your faithfulness and great support in helping this world to be a better place.

To all those who hated and cursed us, who constantly tried to dehumanized and demonized us expecting nothing but failure because you had no hope in you to share with us: don't worry, we forgive you.

References

1. The New English Bible
2. Flavius Josephus—Antiquities of the Jews
3. Marianne Williamson, http://skdesigns.com/internet/articles/quotes/williamson/our_deepest_fear/
4. Bible commentary on Matthew 22:14 http://www.biblegateway.com/resources/commentaries/IVP-NT/Matt/Scorning-Kings-Son
5. *The Road Less Traveled*, M. Scott Peck, MD. http://ghalibana.blogspot.ca/2011/01/my-notes-art-of-loving-by-erich-fromm.html, THE ROAD LESS TRAVELED